MW00533231

BEHIND CLOSED DOORS

ANNA STONE

© 2018 Anna Stone

All rights reserved. No part of this publication may be replicated, reproduced, or redistributed in any form without the prior written consent of the publisher.

This is a work of fiction. Names, characters, places, and incidents either are the products of the author's imagination or are used fictitiously. Any resemblance to actual persons, living or dead, businesses, companies, events, or locales is entirely coincidental.

Cover by Kasmit Covers

ISBN: 9780648419204

EMMA

*E*mma stood on the busy sidewalk and looked up at the skyscraper looming over her. She took a deep breath and entered the lobby.

It was the first day of her new job. But for Emma, it was so much more. It was the start of her new life. Everything was going to plan. She'd found the perfect, surprisingly affordable apartment, and now she was starting the perfect job. She'd signed up for an employment agency when she moved to Chicago a few weeks ago, and they'd finally found her a position. The pay was amazing, and the benefits were even better. She didn't know how she landed such a good job, but she wasn't complaining. And she was not going to mess it up.

Emma scanned the list of businesses next to the elevator. *There.* Avery, Gordon & White. They were on the top floor. The "White" in the law firm's name referred to Lillian White, the woman Emma was going to be working for. Emma wasn't sure what exactly her job entailed; the position was for an assistant of some kind, but the description the agency gave her was vague. It was all very last minute.

Emma rode the elevator up to the top floor and stepped out of it into a wide, open lobby. The firm took up the entire floor. The modern office was almost all white, with marble accents and clean, neat lines. The reception desk was made entirely of marble and had a sign with AG&W written in large black letters behind it. It all felt a bit too artificial to Emma.

The people were much the same. A thin woman with light brown hair sat behind the reception desk. She wore a form-fitting black dress, and her makeup was flawless. A man in a crisp, gray suit with carefully styled hair stood beside the desk, deep in conversation with her. Emma looked down at her own outfit. Her cream-colored blouse, black skirt, and flats were professional enough. But she barely had any makeup on. And she looked nowhere near as stylish as everyone else.

Emma walked over to the desk. As she got closer, the man leaned down toward the woman and quietly said something to her. The woman let out a flirty giggle. The two of them didn't notice Emma until she spoke.

"Hi," Emma said to the woman behind the desk.

The woman smiled. Her teeth seemed unnaturally white. "Can I help you?"

"I'm Emma Cole. Lillian White's new assistant."

The man looked Emma up and down, one eyebrow raised. "You're Lillian's assistant?"

"Yes," Emma said.

"How long do you think this one will last?" he asked the woman.

"Leave her alone, Tom." The woman turned back to Emma. "My name's Bridget, I'm the receptionist. Don't listen to anything Tom here says."

"Someone should warn her," he said. "Don't be fooled by her looks. The interns call her the Ice Queen for a reason."

Emma's stomach fluttered. What kind of woman was she working for? She was suddenly overcome by the feeling that she was out of her depth.

Bridget rolled her eyes. "Ms. White is in a meeting right now, but she's expecting you. You can wait in her office." She pointed to a hall beside the desk. "It's the third office on the left."

"Thanks," Emma said.

Bridget smiled, a little more genuinely this time. "Good luck."

Emma walked down the hall into a large, open office. It was a hive of activity. Every desk was occupied, and phones were ringing constantly. She continued until she came to the third door on the left. The nameplate read *Ms. Lillian White*. Emma opened the door and entered the room.

The office was huge. Two of the walls of the corner office were made entirely of floor-to-ceiling windows. Another wall was covered in tall bookshelves filled with thick tomes. There was a large glass desk at the far end, and some seating around a coffee table to the side.

Emma sat down in front of the desk and looked around. Everything in here was as monochrome and sterile as the lobby, if not more so. She settled into her seat and waited.

After a few minutes, the door swung open and a slender blonde woman walked through.

Lillian White. She was breathtaking. Her light hair was

3

pulled back into a neat bun, and her lips had a pink sheen. She wore a dark gray dress, and heels that made her slender legs seem even longer. She had an effortlessly feminine, delicate beauty. But it was clear that Lillian was anything but delicate. Her face wore a hard expression, and her pale blue eyes shone with ice-cold focus.

Lillian strode into the room, a mug of coffee in one hand, her phone held up to her ear with the other. She didn't even glance at Emma as she made her way to her desk.

"Listen to me," Lillian said. "Do not accept that settlement." She paused. "I don't give a damn how much it is. Don't accept anything less than what we discussed."

Emma stared intently at the hem of her skirt, pretending that she wasn't listening to Lillian's conversation. But she was mesmerized by her commanding voice.

"William. Here's what's going to happen. You're going to reject the offer. You're going to sit patiently and wait while they sweat it out. Then, they're going to come back with another offer. And you know what you're going to do?"

Lillian paused while the man replied.

"No. You're going to reject that offer too. And then they're going to come back and offer what we originally asked for. Then, you can accept. Do you understand? Good." Lillian hung up the phone.

Without saying a word to Emma, Lillian sat down in the high-backed leather chair behind her desk. She took a sip of her coffee, then grimaced. Finally, she looked at Emma.

"Who are you, and what are you doing in my office?" Lillian asked.

"I'm your new assistant," Emma said.

Lillian's eyes swept over Emma. "Is your name Emma Ward?"

"No, it's—"

"Are you fifty-six years old?"

"No."

"Then you're not my new legal assistant."

"My name is Emma Cole. Maybe there was a mix-up?" She should have known this job was too good to be true.

"Obviously," Lillian said. "I'm going to call the agency."

Emma sat and waited while Lillian dialed the number of the agency. Lillian stood up and paced behind her desk. When someone answered, Lillian began to speak to them as if Emma weren't even in the room.

It soon became clear that Emma was right. This was all a mistake.

"I don't want to hear your excuses. How are you going to fix this?" Lillian asked. "Then send me someone else."

Emma's stomach dropped. She was back to where she was a couple of weeks ago. Unemployed and with zero prospects, not to mention zero money. She would have to move back to her hometown. Back to her family. Back to living next door to her ex-fiancé, the man she'd practically left at the altar.

Emma was not giving up on her new life. Not yet.

"What do you mean?" Lillian paused. "That's because everyone you send is incompetent." She raised her hand to her forehead and rubbed her temples. "Then I'll have to look elsewhere." Lillian hung up the phone.

Emma shifted in her seat. A tense silence filled the room.

"There was a clerical error," Lillian said. "Apparently, Emma Ward is no longer with the agency. Your file got switched with hers." Lillian sat back down. "You might as well go. This wasn't your fault, so you'll be compensated. Two weeks' salary should be enough." Lillian opened her laptop again and started to type.

Emma hesitated. Two weeks at the generous rate she was supposed to be paid would tide her over for a while. But still—

"You're still here," Lillian said.

Emma crossed her arms. "You're not even going to give me a chance?"

Lillian stopped typing. "Excuse me?"

"You still need an assistant, don't you?"

"I need a legal assistant."

"I can do that." Emma didn't admit that she had no idea what a legal assistant did.

Lillian appeared to think for a moment. "Fine. Since you're already here, why don't you tell me about yourself? Your qualifications. Your experience." She folded her hands on the desk in front of her.

"I, uh…" Emma didn't usually get tongue-tied. But there was something about Lillian that made her feel off-balance. And she wasn't expecting a job interview on her first day. She thought she already had the job.

"Where did you go to college?" Lillian asked.

"I didn't. Well, I went to community college."

Lillian's lips pressed into a fine line. "Where did you work before this?"

"I was a secretary at a doctor's office for a while. But only part-time because I was studying."

"How old are you?"

"Twenty-seven," Emma said.

"What have you been doing with your life this entire time?"

"Looking after my family. It's just my mom at home, and I have four younger brothers and sisters, so I spent most of the last ten years taking care of them. It kept me pretty busy."

Lillian leaned back in her chair, examining Emma with her piercing eyes. "Are you familiar with legal shorthand?"

"No."

"What about basic legal terminology?"

"No, but—"

"Do you have experience using legal research databases?"

"No."

Lillian pressed her lips together. "What exactly can you do?"

"I can type. Answer phones. Transcribe dictation." Emma could tell that Lillian was not impressed. "And I'm a fast learner. Whatever you need me to do, I can learn it."

"Why do you want this job so badly?" Lillian asked. "I'm sure the agency can find you a position more suitable to someone of your experience level."

"Because I like a challenge." It was the only answer Emma could think of that didn't sound desperate. "And I know that I can do it if you give me a chance."

Lillian sighed. "I was supposed to be getting an experienced legal assistant, but I suppose you can at least cover my admin work. You have until Friday. If you manage to impress me, the job is yours."

Emma nodded. "Okay. Thank you."

"You can address me as Ms. White."

"Yes, Ms. White."

"Good. Now." Lillian picked up a couple of fat files from the top of the stack on her desk. "I need these copied in triplicate." She scribbled something on a sticky note and stuck it on top of the file. "Send a copy each to these two addresses and file the other one. Can you handle that?"

"Yes, Ms. White," Emma replied. Obviously, Lillian thought very little of her. Emma would have to prove her wrong.

"I'll send you an email with further tasks for you to complete today." Lillian turned back to her laptop. "Shut the door behind you."

Emma left the room and let out a long, hard breath. Her heart was racing. She had no idea why she was so flustered.

As she stood there outside Lillian's office, she realized that she didn't know where the photocopier was. Or where anything else was for that matter. And she wasn't going to ask Lillian. She wandered back out to the lobby where Bridget sat behind the desk typing away. The brown-haired woman looked up at Emma as she approached.

"Bridget? Can you tell me where the photocopier is?" Emma asked.

"Let me guess," Bridget said. "Ms. White dumped a heap of work on you without telling you where anything was?"

Emma nodded.

"She always does that." Bridget got up from behind the desk. "Let me show you. I'll give you a tour of the office while I'm at it. It's never that busy out here anyway."

"Thanks," Emma said.

Bridget showed Emma around, pointing out the important locations. The copy room, the break room, the senior partners' offices. She was surprised to learn that the "Tom" she'd run into at reception was one of the senior partners. His behavior with Bridget seemed unprofessional.

Bridget led Emma to a small desk outside Lillian's office. "This is your desk. Now that you're here, I'll be transferring her calls to you instead of straight to her. Which I'm guessing Ms. White didn't mention either?"

"Nope," Emma said.

"Well, get used to figuring things out yourself, because Ms. White isn't going to be any help. Feel free to ask me if you get stuck though."

"You've been a big help already. Thanks."

"Let me know if you need me." Bridget sashayed off to the reception desk.

Emma sat down at her desk and turned on the computer. This couldn't be that different from her job at the doctor's office. How hard could it be?

She steeled herself. She had a week to prove that she could do this. Emma could already tell that impressing Lillian was going to be hard work.

But she was going to keep this job, no matter what.

2

LILLIAN

*L*illian glanced up at Emma as she left the room. Would Emma even make it to the end of the week?

Lillian had enough to worry about already. AG&W had been in trouble for months. Their finances were deep in the red, and their reputation was in tatters.

And for a firm like theirs, reputation was everything. AG&W represented prominent individuals and corporations, most of whom were wrapped up in nasty lawsuits. They looked to AG&W to make their problems disappear. The last thing those clients needed was for their attorneys to be dealing with scandals of their own.

Lillian rubbed her temples. Her job—her entire career— was on the rocks. If worse came to worst, Lillian could easily find another job, but not one where she was a partner. Besides, her stake in the firm was too high for her to walk away from it. All she could do was try to weather the storm and hope that the ship didn't sink.

Lillian shuffled through the files on her desk. Half of them were routine legal documents that needed to be proofread and mailed out. She made a mental note to give them to Emma. Surely she could manage that.

Lillian would have to try to go easy on Emma. The last thing Lillian wanted was for her to quit. By the sound of things, the agency was not happy about the number of legal assistants Lillian went through, and she doubted they'd be able to find her a replacement. Lillian was very particular about how she liked things done, which was why so many of her old assistants hadn't worked out.

It wasn't like she needed someone particularly experienced. She did most of the legal legwork herself or relied on the firm's paralegals and junior lawyers. All she wanted in an assistant was someone assigned to her exclusively to whom she could toss whatever work she needed done. Someone who was good at following her instructions. At the very least, Emma seemed determined and eager to please. Perhaps there was potential in her.

Lillian had to admit, she found Emma refreshing. She seemed much more down-to-earth than most of the people who worked at AG&W. With her dark chestnut hair and big hazel eyes, she had that quintessential girl-next-door look, which made her stand out in an office full of straitlaced men and women in expensive suits.

Lillian turned back to her laptop and opened a browser window. Immediately, the computer froze. She cursed. Today was not her day. She looked at her watch. It was almost time for the weekly partners' meeting. Abandoning her frozen laptop, Lillian left her office.

She stopped by the bathroom on the way. One of the perks of being the only female partner was that she had the women's executive bathroom to herself. Lillian stood in front of the mirror and freed her hair from its tight bun. She didn't like the plain hairstyle, but it made her look more respectable. Lillian's entire look—from her subtle, natural makeup to her pantsuits and business-appropriate dresses—was carefully curated to make her appear as professional as possible without sacrificing her femininity.

She was a pretty, blonde woman with a name that sounded like it belonged on a perfume bottle. People had a hard time taking someone who looked like her seriously. Especially the men in her profession, half of whom seemed to be stuck in the 1950s regardless of how old they were. It had the benefit of making people underestimate her, which she'd used to her advantage. But after over a decade of practicing law at AG&W, every lawyer in the city knew her. And they knew better than to underestimate Lillian White.

Lillian grabbed her hairbrush from the counter, ran it through her hair, and put it back into a bun, looser this time. She left the bathroom and made her way to the meeting room.

When she arrived, Michael Avery, the "A" in AG&W, was already inside. Avery, as he preferred to be called, and Thomas Gordon Sr. were the founding partners. After Gordon retired, Avery became the managing partner, giving him the bulk of the responsibility when it came to the firm.

Lillian had always been certain that Avery was the reason she'd made partner at the exceptionally young age of twenty-eight. He had been her mentor from the day she started working at the firm as an intern, and had taken her under his wing and taught her everything she knew. He was one of the few people who saw past her looks to her potential.

It had been six years since Lillian became partner, and as she'd evolved from Avery's protege to his peer, she learned that he, too, was more than he appeared. On the surface, he was friendly and charismatic, and the complete opposite of Lillian. One flash of his confident smile and clients would trust him with their lives. But he didn't become one of the most powerful attorneys in the city because of his good nature and trustworthiness. He was a wolf disguised as a Labrador.

Lillian watched him for a moment through the door. He was examining some documents, his brows knitted and his eyes narrowed. Recently, his black hair and beard had started to show flecks of gray, and the lines in his face had deepened. With his solemn expression and his dark suit, Lillian was struck with the impression that he was at a funeral.

"Good morning, Lillian," Avery said when she entered the room. "How was your weekend?"

Lillian didn't know why he still bothered to ask her about her weekend. She hadn't had a weekend off in months, and neither had he. "You want to know how my weekend was, Avery? I spent most of it working on that antitrust case. Junior was supposed to analyze the discovery documents, but he did such a sloppy job that I had to do it myself."

"You know how much he hates being called Junior."

"And I don't like being called the Ice Queen, but that doesn't stop him from spreading that childish nickname to the interns."

Before Avery could respond, Thomas Gordon Jr. walked through the doorway, his hands in the pockets of his designer suit. His light brown hair was parted carefully to the side. Lillian had never met a man as vain as him. If only he put as much effort into his work as he did his appearance.

Thomas was the perfect example of nepotism in action. His father, Thomas Gordon Sr., was the original "Gordon" in AG&W and part of the reason the firm was in such bad shape. About a year ago, Gordon had been accused of sexual harassment by one of their employees who claimed that he had coerced her into becoming his mistress. Gordon hadn't denied the relationship but claimed that everything was consensual. Considering his long history of sleazy behavior in the office, Lillian had no doubt that he was guilty.

The ensuing lawsuit had made national news. In the end, it had been settled out of court and cost the firm millions. Gordon had agreed to retire early; however, his "voluntary" resignation had come with the caveat that his son replaced him as partner. Lillian and Avery had no choice but to agree to his terms. To top it off, Lillian and Avery later discovered that Gordon had been mismanaging the firm's finances.

"Good morning, Thomas," Avery said. "Take a seat."

Thomas sat down a couple of seats away from Lillian and stretched out lazily in his chair. He turned to address her. "I met your new assistant out there. Emma, wasn't it? She's pretty easy on the eyes. I hope you keep this one."

Lillian didn't respond. Ever since Thomas found out that Lillian was a lesbian, he'd taken to voicing his crude opinions about women's appearances. She didn't know what he hoped to accomplish.

"Thomas," Avery said. "We've spoken about this. You need to stop behaving inappropriately when it comes to our female employees. Even if there's nothing serious going on, it's not a good look for the firm. The entire office has seen you flirting with the receptionist, for God's sake."

"We're just messing around. It's some harmless fun, that's all."

"That's exactly what your father said about all the women he sexually harassed," Lillian said.

Thomas's expression darkened. Before he could respond, Avery cut him off.

"Look." Avery shot Lillian a stern glance. "The last thing we need right now is another scandal. All of us need to keep our noses clean." He opened the folder in front of him. "Let's move on to business."

The meeting didn't get any better from there. Avery informed them that the firm would no longer be paying for unnecessary travel expenses. No more business-class flights or five-star hotel rooms. Lillian didn't mind. She could afford to pay for those kinds of things out of her own pocket. And she was relieved that Avery didn't suggest "downsizing." It meant that the firm wasn't in dire straits yet.

The conversation moved on to other matters. When Avery was done with the last item on his list, Thomas stood up and put his hands in his pockets.

"Are we done here?" he asked.

"Yes," Avery said. "Unless you have anything to add, Lillian?"

"No," Lillian replied. "Don't let us keep you, Thomas."

"Lillian, a moment." Avery waited as Thomas left the room. "You need to stop antagonizing Thomas. That comment about his father was out of line."

"Do you expect me to sit back and listen to his sexist drivel?" Avery was the only person Lillian let admonish her like that.

"I expect you to behave professionally and treat Thomas with respect."

"I'll respect him when he respects the women of the office. And when he starts doing his goddamn job."

"Lillian. Thomas is a partner now," Avery said. "I know you don't like it. But we have to make the best of this. AG&W is hanging by a thread. I worked too hard to build this firm to have it fall apart because the two of you are at each other's throats. All our careers are on the line here, including yours."

"Fine." Lillian held her hands up in defeat. "I'll play nice. But don't expect the two of us to be friends."

"That's good enough for me. I'm going to go talk to Thomas." Avery left the room.

Lillian doubted Avery's conversation with Thomas would go well. Thomas seemed to despise Lillian even more than Lillian disliked him.

Lillian stood up. She had plenty of work to do. Hopefully, this new assistant of hers wouldn't be entirely useless.

3

EMMA

*E*mma shook the last few drops of coffee out of the cup and into her mouth, then threw it into the bin next to her desk. She had somehow made it through her first day. Lillian had given her basic tasks, seemingly convinced that Emma was unable to handle anything difficult. She did have to ask for Bridget's help a few times, but she was slowly learning the ropes. At the end of the day, Lillian had sent her home, instructing her to study legal terminology and abbreviations. That had to be a good sign.

It was her second day working for Lillian, and Emma had come into the office early before Lillian arrived to do said studying on her work computer. A mix-up with the cable company meant that the internet at her apartment wasn't connected yet, so she hadn't had a chance to look anything up last night.

Over the top of her monitor, Emma saw Lillian walking toward her. God, she was stunning. She wore a pantsuit today, one that looked like it was tailored to fit every one of her curves, and matte-black heels that clicked on the smooth, white floor with every footstep. And the way Lillian walked… It was like she owned the room and everything and everyone in it. Emma supposed she did, in a way.

Lillian stopped in front of Emma's desk. "What are you doing here so early?"

"My apartment doesn't have an internet connection yet. I wanted to do some research on legal terms. Is that okay?"

"I don't see why not," Lillian said. "Come see me at 8 a.m."

"Yes, Ms. White," Emma replied. But Lillian was already halfway to her office.

Emma looked at the clock on her screen. She had just enough time to grab another coffee from the place down the street. The coffee in the breakroom left a lot to be desired.

She made her way out of the building and down the few blocks to the coffee shop. It was packed full of corporate types from the surrounding offices. It seemed like everyone around here ran on coffee, Lillian included.

Emma reached the head of the line and ordered herself a latte. As she pulled out her wallet to pay, she decided to add a large black coffee to her order. Lillian was constantly drinking coffee. It couldn't hurt to get on her good side. It could be the difference between keeping this job or not.

As she waited for her order, Bridget, the receptionist sidled up beside her, looking just as stylish and photo-perfect as yesterday.

Bridget smiled. "Good to see that you came back."

"Why wouldn't I?" Emma asked.

"Well, it's no secret that Ms. White isn't the easiest person to work for. If you quit, you wouldn't be the first."

"How many assistants has Lillian had?" Surely she wasn't that bad.

"That depends. Do the ones that only lasted a couple of days count?"

The barista called out Emma's name, then Bridget's shortly after. Coffee in hand, they left the coffee shop, joining the stream of pedestrians heading in the direction of the office.

"So, what happened to Ms. White's old assistants?" Emma asked.

"Let's see. She fired a few of them, mostly for stupid mistakes like sending out a letter with a typo in it. The others quit in the first couple of weeks. Couldn't take the heat." Bridget must have noticed the nervous expression on Emma's face. "But I'm sure you'll be able to handle it."

Emma got a feeling that the other Emma who was supposed to be here was far more experienced than her. But she didn't say anything.

They entered the lobby and rode the elevator up to the AG&W offices. By the time Emma got back to her desk, it was 8 a.m. exactly. With Lillian's coffee in her hand, Emma went to knock on Lillian's door. Lillian always kept her door closed to prevent unnecessary interruptions.

"Come in," Lillian said.

Emma approached Lillian's desk and placed the cup of coffee on it. "I brought you coffee. I know you drink it black, but I wasn't sure if you take sugar."

"You're not my personal assistant," Lillian said, not

looking up from the papers she was working on. "I don't want you wasting time running errands for me."

"It was in my own time." Emma crossed her arms. Here she was, trying to do something nice, and Lillian basically took it as an insult. "I was getting coffee for myself, and I thought you might want one."

Lillian put down her pen and gave Emma a frosty stare.

Whoops. Although Lillian never said anything, Emma got the impression that she expected her assistant to keep her mouth shut unless spoken to, like an old-fashioned schoolmistress. Emma hoped her mouth wouldn't get her in trouble. "It's much better than the breakroom coffee," she added sheepishly.

After a moment, Lillian picked up the coffee and took a sip. "Thank you."

Emma hid a smile. Lillian's thanks had sounded stilted, but it was something. And maybe Emma's reasons for wanting to impress Lillian weren't entirely job-related. Emma felt a compulsion to please her for reasons that she didn't quite understand.

Emma didn't get to bask in Lillian's gratitude for long.

"I have a lot of work for you today," Lillian said. "You're going to need to write this down."

Emma whipped out a pen and notepad. She had come prepared. Lillian listed off a number of tasks, from simple things like more photocopying to more complicated things like transcribing Lillian's notes.

"I don't care how long it takes you," Lillian said. "Just make sure your transcription is accurate and error-free. Look up the abbreviations if you need to. Start on that first."

"Yes, Ms. White."

Emma got to work. As soon as she started, she was glad that Lillian had told her to take her time. The handwritten notes were full of abbreviations and shorthand, and she ended up spending half her time looking them up. After working for two hours straight, Emma had memorized the common ones. And once she began to understand what she was transcribing, she started to enjoy herself. The cases within were actually interesting.

Around lunchtime, she delivered the transcribed notes to Lillian, who responded with nothing more than a murmur of acknowledgment. Emma still had a lot to do, all while handling Lillian's phone calls.

Around midafternoon, Emma returned to her desk after a bathroom break. As soon as she sat down, her phone rang. It was Lillian, summoning Emma into her office.

"Yes, Ms. White?" Emma said.

"Where have you been?" Lillian asked. "I've been calling your desk for ten minutes."

"I was in the bathroom," Emma said. "Most of the stalls are out of order, so there was a line." Bridget said they had been out of order for weeks. But there were only a few women in the office, most of whom held secretarial roles, so their requests to get it fixed fell on deaf ears.

Lillian frowned. "I'll get that taken care of. For now, I want you to use my bathroom. I'm the only female partner so I'm the only other person who uses it. I can't have you disappearing all the time."

"Yes, Ms. White."

"That's not why I called you in here." Lillian's voice had a sterner than usual edge to it.

Emma's stomach sank. Had she made a mistake?

Lillian pushed a file toward her. "What is this?"

Emma opened the folder. "These are the notes I tran-scribed this morning."

"Turn to page four. Third line. What does it say?"

Emma flipped to the page and located the sentence. "The employer agreed to receive a fifty-thousand-dollar settle-ment..." Emma frowned. That wasn't right.

"EE stands for employee. *ER* is short for employer. That's not the only sentence where you mixed up those two abbreviations."

"I'm sorry, Ms. White," Emma said. Was this it? Was she fired?

"Just go fix it."

Emma looked up in surprise. "You're not going to fire me?"

"No, I'm not." Lillian sat back in her chair and folded her hands in her lap. "Why do you think I would fire you over something like this?"

"No reason," Emma said quickly.

"You've been listening to rumors, Emma," Lillian said, the slightest hint of amusement in her voice. "Don't believe everything you hear."

Emma nodded.

"For the record, if I were going to fire you, I wouldn't bother telling you what you did wrong. You'd be out the door already. I'm telling you because I want you to learn from it. Be more careful next time."

"Yes, Ms. White." Emma lingered by the desk. "Is there anything else?"

"No. That's all."

Emma returned to her desk, her pulse racing. Was it because she thought she was going to be fired? Or was it something else? Something about Lillian?

Whatever the reason, Emma had never felt anything like the way she did right now.

4

EMMA

*O*n Friday morning, Emma dragged herself into the office. Like every other day that week, she'd stayed past 5 p.m. the day before until Lillian had told her to leave. She had so much work to do. Lillian had Emma transcribe both her handwritten notes and her dictation. Lillian dictated everything because it was more efficient. She was all about efficiency. Luckily, that was the one skill Emma possessed from working at the doctor's office that Lillian seemed pleased about.

On top of all of this, Emma was still studying up on legal procedure in her own time. She was determined not to make a mistake like the last one. So far, she hadn't made any major errors. But Lillian was a perfectionist. Emma lost track of the number of times Lillian had sent her back to her desk to fix a document. *This should be justified. This should be in italics, not underlined. These names should be written out in full.* And Emma would just nod, and say "Yes, Ms. White," and then fix whatever minor imperfection Lillian had found without complaint.

Lillian seemed impossible to satisfy. It made it difficult for Emma to tell whether she was doing a good job or not. And she only had one day left to prove herself.

Emma wasn't at all surprised when Lillian called her back into her office just half an hour after their 8 a.m. coffee and brief.

"Emma," Lillian said. "Take a look at this and tell me what's wrong with it."

Emma took the document from Lillian. It was a contract that Emma had drafted from Lillian's dictation. She had made sure to follow Lillian's detailed instructions on the layout and formatting.

Emma scanned the page. "I'm not sure what the problem is."

"Second paragraph, third sentence."

Emma located the sentence in question. "Uh…" Emma still couldn't see what was wrong with it.

"What did I tell you about commas?" Lillian asked.

Right. "To use Oxford commas. To put a comma before the word 'and' at the end of a list."

"So, what's wrong with that sentence?"

"There should be a comma after the word 'state.'" Emma said. "I'll fix it right away."

"Before you do that." Lillian typed something into her laptop. "I want you to read something. Sit down."

Emma sat in one of the chairs in front of Lillian's desk.

Lillian stood up and brought the laptop over to Emma's side of the desk. "Read this."

Emma leaned in and looked at what was on the screen. It was an article about a case. *O'Connor v. Oakhurst Dairy.* Lillian leaned back against her desk and crossed one ankle over the other. Her casual body language seemed so unlike the stiff 'Ms. White' Emma knew. She began to read. It was hard to concentrate with Lillian watching her with those pale eyes. Emma's skin tingled.

"Are you finished?" Lillian asked.

"Yes," Emma replied.

"Explain the case to me. In your own words."

"A group of truck drivers filed a class-action suit against their employer for overtime pay. Oakhurst Dairy lost the lawsuit because their employment contract didn't contain Oxford commas. As a result, one of the clauses was deemed to be ambiguous, so the company was ordered to pay the drivers a ten-million-dollar settlement." It was an extreme example of a typo costing a client millions.

"Very good," Lillian said. She reached out and shut the laptop. "I asked you to read this because I want you to understand that I'm not being pedantic. I'll never ask you to do something for no reason."

Emma nodded.

"Now go and fix that document."

"Yes, Ms. White." Emma got up to leave.

"Wait. Sit back down," Lillian said.

Emma sat back down obediently.

"You're very good at following my instructions. Most people who work for me end up resenting being ordered around all the time. But it doesn't seem to bother you."

Emma shrugged. "I don't mind."

"Do you still want to work for me?"

"Yes," Emma replied.

"Why? This job isn't easy as I'm sure you're aware by now."

"Because I like the challenge," Emma said.

"Yes, you said that already. This isn't a job interview. I'm not judging you on what you say. Why do you really want to work for me?"

"Well, I really need a job at the moment," Emma admitted. "But I really do like working for you."

"What do you like about it?" Lillian asked.

Emma wasn't sure what to say. "It's interesting. The work, I mean."

Lillian's lips curled up slightly. She folded her arms over her chest. "Are you sure that's the only reason you like working for me?"

Heat spread up Emma's cheeks. "I don't understand what you mean."

Lillian studied Emma silently for a moment. Then she turned back to her laptop. "Forget I said anything."

Emma left the room without waiting to be dismissed. *What was that about?* Pulling herself together, she sat down at her desk and finished off her coffee. As she returned to her work, she realized that Lillian hadn't told her whether she had the job or not. But it was still early in the day.

She was glad the weekend was coming up because she needed the time to recuperate. Then she remembered she'd promised her mom that she'd go home for the weekend to check up on things and help out, but Emma didn't think she could make the two-hour drive without falling asleep at the wheel. Emma would call her mom after work.

She hoped her family would be able to cope without her. It wasn't like they really needed Emma anymore. The kids were all teenagers now, old enough to take care of themselves. Plus, her mom had gotten a promotion which left her with more than enough money to hire help if she needed it. That—and the fact that her ex-fiancé lived next door to them—was why Emma had finally moved out. But she still worried about her family, her mom most of all. The kids weren't the only ones who needed looking after.

Emma sighed. She could worry about that later.

Hours passed, and Emma's list of tasks grew shorter. Five o'clock rolled around but went unnoticed by most of the employees. Hardly anyone at the office left on time, and Emma was no exception. An hour later, Emma finished off the last of the work Lillian had given her and went to Lillian's office to check in.

"Here are those files you asked for," Emma said. "They've all been proofread. And I sent out those demand letters."

"Did you type up the notes for the Brenner deposition?" Lillian asked.

"Yes. And I fixed some errors too."

"What errors?"

"The date was wrong in a couple of places. It said December of this year instead of last year. I figured someone made a mistake. That is, unless the case was filed in the future," she joked.

Lillian frowned. Emma realized too late that the someone who made the mistake was probably Lillian. She wasn't doing a very good job of keeping her mouth shut.

"Good," Lillian said. "You can go home now."

Emma hovered before Lillian's desk.

"Do you want something?"

"It's Friday," Emma said. "You said I had till the end of the week to prove that I could handle the job."

Silence hung in the air. Emma wondered if Lillian was only now making her decision.

"I want you here at 8 a.m. sharp on Monday," Lillian finally said.

Emma nodded. "Yes, Ms. White."

"Goodbye, Emma."

Emma smiled to herself as she left Lillian's office.

Emma entered her apartment and threw herself down onto the couch, coat, purse, and all. Her excitement about keeping her job had faded once she remembered that she had to call her mom to tell her she wouldn't be coming home this weekend. Her mom wouldn't hold it against her, but she'd be sad. When they had spoken earlier in the week, she had been looking forward to Emma's visit.

Emma picked up her phone and dialed her mom's number. After a dozen rings, her mom picked up the phone.

"Hi, Mom," Emma said.

"Emma, it's good to hear your voice," her mom said.

"How are things at home?"

"It's a madhouse. The twins are brawling in the living room, Lisa is whining because Margo won't talk to her, and Margo is sulking because of some boy. So business as usual."

Emma smiled. Despite everything, she missed home. She missed the activity, the chaos. Her one-bedroom apartment felt too quiet in comparison. Too empty. She hadn't had a chance to decorate it, so it didn't feel lived in yet. And she still didn't know many people in Chicago. It was a little lonely.

"How've you been doing?" Emma asked her mom.

"I'm fine, honey."

"Have you been keeping up your appointments with Dr. Holden?"

"Yes. You don't have to remind me every time you call."

"I just worry about you," Emma said.

"I know. But you don't have to," her mom said. "That's enough about me. How are you? How's the job?"

"I'm good. The job is going well. My boss is very... demanding. I've been working overtime every day this week."

"Don't let her work you too hard."

Emma almost laughed at the thought of having any control over what Lillian demanded of her.

There was loud yelling in the background on the other end of the line.

"That's just the twins. I'll deal with them when I get off the phone." Emma's mom sighed. "Justin has been a handful lately. He's been acting up a lot."

"I'll talk to him," Emma said. Just because she'd moved out didn't mean that she wasn't still their big sister. Even before her father had died ten years ago, she'd been playing the role of extra parent to her much younger siblings. And she was far better at handling her teenage brothers' and sisters' moods than her mom. Probably because Emma still remembered what it was like to be a teenager.

"Thanks," her mom said. "I was never good with boys. Your dad, he was the one who knew how to handle them. He used to entertain his nephews for hours." Her mom's voice took on that wistful quality that it always did when she spoke about Emma's dad.

"I remember," Emma said.

"He was the one who wanted boys in the first place. I wish he'd gotten to see them grow up."

"Me too," Emma said. Her mom had been bringing up her dad a lot more lately, which was never a good sign.

"Was there a reason you called?" her mom asked.

"Yes. I can't make it back there this weekend."

"Oh. That's okay, honey."

Emma could hear the disappointment in her mom's voice even though she tried to hide it. "I've been really busy with my new job. I need some time to recharge."

"Emma, it's fine. Don't worry about it," she said.

Someone shouted in the background again. Emma pulled the phone away from her ear.

Her mom sighed. "I should go make sure the twins aren't killing each other. I'll talk to you later."

"Okay. I'll call you in a couple of days. Look after yourself, Mom."

Emma hung up the phone, then sprawled out on the couch. She had no intention of leaving it for the rest of the weekend. She smiled to herself. Despite the exhaustion, she liked her job. It was all new and exciting.

And she liked working for Lillian. Everything about Lillian captivated her. Her unyielding strength. Her pale blue eyes, which at times seemed ice cold, and at other times seemed to burn like a dangerously hot flame. Her perfect, pink lips...

It was at that moment that Emma realized exactly what she'd been feeling toward Lillian all this time.

5

LILLIAN

*L*illian entered the restaurant. She was a regular here, along with most of the people in the room. It was the venue of choice for the city's elite businessmen, execs, and lawyers to hold "business meetings." Wining and dining clients tended to make them much more amenable.

However, today her lunch was personal. Lillian only had an hour before she had to get back to work, but it was a welcome change from being stuck in the office. She spotted her friend, a tall, red-haired woman, sitting at a table by the far window.

"Chelsea," Lillian sat down across from her. "Good to see you."

"Likewise," Chelsea said.

Chelsea and Lillian had been friends since law school. They'd been having these monthly lunches for years. Chelsea was the head of in-house counsel at a large property development firm, so her job was just as high pressure as Lillian's. They both appreciated the chance to de-stress and vent about everything that came with their respective lives.

"How was the honeymoon?" Lillian asked. Chelsea had just gotten married to the love of her life, a man named Ryan. Personally, Lillian found him insufferable. But for some reason, he made Chelsea happy, which was good enough for Lillian.

"It was pure bliss." Chelsea sighed. "Coming back to work after two weeks of relaxation in the Greek Islands was hell. Apparently, the legal department is useless without me. I've spent most of this week cleaning up everyone's messes."

A waiter approached the table and took their orders. Lillian ordered a glass of wine to go with her lunch.

"How are things at AG&W?" Chelsea asked. "Is the new partner still causing problems?"

"Don't get me started on Thomas. I had to cover his ass because he didn't show up for a meeting with a client yesterday. He was off having a drink at some country club and lost track of time."

"He sounds charming."

"I've got my hands full right now. The last thing I need is to waste my time babysitting him. I just picked up a new client—a manufacturing firm. The CEO is a kid who inherited his company from his father. He's definitely involved in some shady dealings behind the scenes. I hope he isn't stupid enough to tell me about them. He's a real scumbag."

"When did you grow a conscience?" Chelsea asked. "You've been working with clients like him for years without batting an eye."

"I don't know why it's bothering me." When Lillian first started practicing law, she quickly learned to throw her principles out the window. She had to in order to advance her career. Nowadays, she was able to pick and choose her clients, so she turned down the most immoral of cases. But she wasn't exactly working for the good guys. "It just seems like lately every single client that comes my way is an arrogant asshole who believes if they throw enough money at me, I'll make all their problems go away. They think that the law doesn't apply to them."

"Do I sense a midlife crisis coming on?"

"Very funny. I'm still in my thirties, Chelsea," Lillian said. "It doesn't matter. I'm probably just stressed out from all the chaos at work. The firm still hasn't recovered from Gordon Sr."

"You know, you can always come work with me."

"Once again, I'll have to pass," Lillian said. "I'd be bored out of my mind with all the paperwork. And I'd never see the inside of a courtroom again." Even now, she rarely got to go to court. Most of the cases she worked on were settled before they even made it in front of a judge. She missed taking cases to trial.

"And your ego couldn't handle not having your name on the building?" Chelsea asked.

"That too."

The conversation halted as their food arrived, along with Lillian's drink. She took a long sip, understanding why so many attorneys were functional alcoholics.

"So," Lillian said. "I have a new legal assistant."

"Oh? And how long until you fire this one?"

"I only fired one. The others quit," Lillian said. "I actually did consider firing her at first. She wasn't even supposed to be working for me. The agency sent her by mistake. But I've decided to keep her on and train her myself."

Lillian had quickly realized that Emma's lack of experience was an advantage. She didn't have years of bad habits that Lillian would have to fix like her previous assistants. And she turned out to be more capable than Lillian had expected. She learned quickly and had an eye for detail.

"She's perfect for the role. She seems completely impervious to my demands. I could tell her to stand on one leg and hop in a circle and she'd probably do it without complaint."

"So what you're saying is that you've found someone who will put up with your ridiculously high standards and isn't fazed by the fact that you're impossible to satisfy?" Chelsea asked. "Sounds like you've met your match."

"She seems too good to be true. But there's something about her that makes me wonder if she's really as obedient as she pretends to be."

"Lillian," Chelsea said. "Don't even think about it."

"What?" Lillian asked.

"I can see it in your eyes. And I know your type."

"I don't know what you're talking about, Chelsea."

"I've known you since college," Chelsea said. "Do you think I can't tell when you're lying?"

"You have nothing to worry about. I would never go there. I won't take advantage of someone who works for me. Besides, after everything with Gordon Sr., we made some pretty strict rules about office relationships. I wouldn't put my job at risk like that."

"Don't say I didn't warn you," Chelsea said.

"Where the hell is Thomas?" Lillian said to no one in particular. She hadn't even been back in the office for five minutes, and she was back to dealing with his shit. She stormed out to the reception desk. Sure enough, Thomas was flirting shamelessly with Bridget.

"Thomas," Lillian said. "My office. Now."

Thomas turned to Lillian, his jaw clenched. "Do you think I'm one of the interns? You can't just order me around like that."

"I don't think you want us to have this conversation here," Lillian said.

Thomas glanced around the room. He turned back to Bridget. "Sorry Bridget, duty calls."

Lillian headed to her office and sat at her desk. Moments later, Thomas appeared.

"What the hell, Lillian?" he said. "You can't speak to me like that in front of everyone."

"I wouldn't have to if you did your goddamn job," Lillian said.

Thomas glared at her. "What's this about?"

Lillian gestured toward a chair in front of her desk. "Take a seat."

Thomas sat down on the chair, slouching in it like a rebellious schoolboy.

Lillian reached into her briefcase and produced a document. She threw it onto the desk in front of her. "What the hell is this?"

Thomas leaned over and glanced at the front page. "The discovery plan for the Jones & Welsch case."

"The one that you were supposed to put together?"

"Yes."

"Then why does it read like it was written by a first-year law student who can barely speak English?"

Thomas shrugged. "I don't see anything wrong with it."

"If that's true, either you haven't read it, or you're more incompetent than I thought. Which is it?"

Thomas's face clouded over. "I didn't write it myself, okay? I gave it to one of the interns to do. That's what they're here for after all."

"No, that's not what they're here for." Lillian folded her hands on the desk. "I don't care what you do with your own cases. But when you're on a case with me, I expect you to do your own work." Lillian tore up the document and dropped it in the trash can next to her desk. "You're going to rewrite this. And you're going to bring it to me by the end of the day."

Thomas raised an eyebrow. "Or what?"

"Do not test me, Thomas."

Seconds passed in silence as they stared each other down. Thomas's face darkened with every passing moment.

There was a knock at the door.

"Come in, Emma," Lillian said, her eyes never leaving Thomas's.

Emma opened the door. "Ms. White—" Emma noticed Thomas in the chair and stopped in her tracks. "Sorry, I can come back."

"Stay. Thomas was just leaving."

"This isn't over, Lillian." Thomas got up from his chair and walked toward the door. He stopped in front of Emma and gave her the up-and-down glance that he gave every good-looking woman he crossed paths with. He opened his mouth to speak to her.

Lillian cut him off. "Leave. Now."

Thomas bristled. He shot Lillian a scathing glare. Then, just to spite her, he gave Emma one last look, and left the office.

"I'm sorry," Emma said. "I didn't know you had someone in here."

"It's fine," Lillian said.

"Is everything okay? Things seemed pretty tense in here."

"It's nothing. That poor excuse for a lawyer is the bane of my existence, that's all," Lillian said. "I'm sorry if he made you uncomfortable."

"It's okay." Emma said.

"No, it's not. He was looking at you like you were a piece of meat." It bothered Lillian much more than it should have.

A faint blush rose up Emma's cheeks. "I appreciate the concern, but it's fine." She placed a folder on Lillian's desk. "I tracked down those files for you."

"Good," Lillian said. "I emailed you some documents. I need you to proofread them and send them back to me."

"Right away, Ms. White," Emma said with a smile.

Lillian watched her leave. Chelsea may have had a point. There was something about Emma that Lillian found enticing. Was it her sweet disposition? That teasing smile of hers? The way she would say "Ms. White," as if every letter was dipped in honey?

And Lillian's question about why Emma liked working for her hadn't been entirely innocent. It was impulsive, a

41

moment of weakness, and completely unlike Lillian. But she'd wanted to see how Emma would react.

And react she had.

But it didn't matter. Lillian was not going to slip up again.

6

EMMA

*E*mma dumped her things on her desk and turned on her computer. She'd been working at AG&W for weeks now, and time had only confirmed what she'd realized at the end of her first week.

She was head over heels for Lillian White.

She had no idea why she was so drawn to Lillian, considering everything about her seemed to scream "keep away." But there had to be something behind those icy blue eyes. Emma knew it. And she was determined to slip under Lillian's guard.

Emma wondered if she should be more surprised by the fact that she was attracted to women. Well, she was attracted to one woman at least. Wasn't she supposed to have some kind of big, dramatic awakening? Wasn't she supposed to feel conflicted? The only person she'd ever been with was her ex-fiancé, who was a man. Was she a lesbian, or bisexual, or something else?

She didn't know. And right now, she didn't care. All she knew was that whenever she thought about Lillian, it made her pulse race and her skin flush. She wanted so badly to embrace those feelings and find out where they would lead.

If only Lillian weren't her boss.

Emma sighed. She knew she should put all thoughts of pursuing Lillian out of her head. But sometimes she wondered if her infatuation wasn't entirely one-sided. Now and then, she would glance at Lillian and find Lillian looking back at her, a heat in her eyes that set Emma's skin alight.

Emma sighed, then realized she had sighed three times in the past minute. Collecting herself, she made her way to Lillian's office.

"Good morning, Ms. White," Emma said.

"Emma." Lillian glanced at her from over the top of her laptop.

"Here's your coffee." Emma placed the cup on the desk in front of Lillian. It had become part of their morning routine.

"Thank you," Lillian said. She shut her laptop. "How do you feel about working some overtime today, Emma?"

"More overtime than usual, you mean?" The words tumbled out of Emma's mouth before she could stop them.

"I didn't realize you had a problem with me keeping you here after hours."

Emma smiled. "I don't mind at all, Ms. White."

Lillian crossed her arms, her lips pressed into a line. "Something has changed about you. I'm not sure if I like it."

Blood rose to Emma's cheeks. Lillian's tone was firm and scolding, but there was a flicker of heat in her eyes once again. Emma still didn't quite understand what it was.

"Is that a yes to overtime?" Lillian asked.

Emma nodded. "Yes."

"It's the Exco case," Lillian said. "The client has decided to go ahead with arbitration proceedings, which gives us less time to put together a case than I would have liked."

As Lillian continued, Emma's mind began to wander. Late nights alone in the office with Lillian. That could prove difficult. But she was a grown woman. Surely she could behave herself.

"Do you think you can handle it?"

"Yes." Emma hadn't even heard half of what Lillian had said.

"Good. Finish up what you were working on yesterday, then come see me and we can get started."

"Right away, Ms. White."

"Emma?" Lillian said.

"Yes?"

"Call me Lillian."

Around 8 p.m. that night, Emma returned to the office carrying a bag of takeout. She knocked on Lillian's door.

"Come in," Lillian said.

Lillian sat behind her desk, scribbling away furiously, glancing over at her laptop screen now and then. The desk was an orderly mess of files and papers. Lillian didn't look up at Emma at all. At some point while Emma was gone, Lillian had freed her long blonde hair from its bun. It fell down over her shoulders like gold-colored silk, framing her face and softening the angles of her cheekbones and chin.

As if on cue, Lillian combed her fingers over her scalp

from front to back, drawing them through her hair. "What is it, Emma?"

Emma hadn't realized she was standing there staring. "I brought you dinner," she said. "It's from the Thai place across the street. I figured you'd be hungry since you didn't eat lunch." Emma had quickly learned that Lillian was the type to forget about normal human functions like eating and sleeping when she was working.

"I didn't know you had time to keep tabs on me." Lillian's eyes remained fixed on the screen. "I should be giving you more work to do."

"Here." Emma placed the bag down on Lillian's desk. "You really shouldn't skip meals so often," she said under her breath.

"Are you forgetting which of us is in charge here?"

"Sorry," Emma said.

Lillian sighed. "No, I suppose you're right. I'll eat something once I've sent off this email."

"Can I stay and eat with you, then?"

Lillian finally looked up at Emma. "Why not? Go sit down by the coffee table and I'll join you in a minute."

Emma walked over to the coffee table and set the food down, opening the boxes one by one. A spicy aroma filled the air. After a few minutes, Lillian shut her laptop, walked over to the coffee table, and sat down across from Emma. Once Emma started to eat, she realized how hungry she was.

After a few mouthfuls, Lillian set her fork down. "I hope all this overtime isn't keeping you from anything."

"Nope," Emma said. "I just moved here. I don't really know anyone or have anything to do other than work."

"No one is waiting up for you at home?"

"No. I live by myself. And I'm completely unattached," Emma added.

"Really? I'd be careful if I were you. If you tell anyone in the office that you're single, you'll have half the men in the building offering to buy you lunch. These high-powered types can't resist a pretty young woman."

"Only the men?" Emma asked, feeling bold.

Lillian sat back and crossed her legs. "And some of the women."

Emma was suddenly aware that the offices outside the door were almost empty. Completely unbidden, an image of Lillian crossing the table and pinning Emma down on the couch filled her mind.

"So, why did you move to Chicago?" Lillian asked.

Emma hesitated. Lillian had never asked her about her personal life before. "I wanted a fresh start," she said. "Well, more like a chance to actually start living. When my dad died ten years ago, I put my life on hold to look after my family. The twins were still toddlers, and Margo, who's the oldest after me, was only six. I stepped in to help raise them. But now that they're older, they don't need me anymore, so I decided it was time for me to try to find my own path." Emma picked at the noodles in front of her. "And there was the fact that my ex-fiancé lived next door. Our families are really close, so when everything ended with him it was hard to avoid seeing each other all the time."

"What happened between the two of you?" Lillian asked.

"It's complicated," Emma replied. "We'd been friends for as long as I could remember. We grew up together. When we got to high school, he kept asking me out, over and over, until I finally said yes. I mean, I did like him. And everyone always assumed that we'd end up together, including both our families, so I just went along with it. A couple of years ago, we got engaged. But I kept pushing the wedding back further and further until I called it all off entirely and finally admitted the truth."

"And that was?" Lillian asked

"That I didn't love him," Emma said. "At least, not in that way. It always felt like there was something missing. But I didn't realize it because I was so used to going through life trying to make everyone else happy that I never stopped to think about what I wanted. That's why I moved away. I wanted time and space to find myself and figure out what I want."

"And? Have you figured out what you want yet?"

"I have a few ideas," Emma replied.

"I hope you find what you're looking for," Lillian said.

The conversation turned to work as they finished off the last of the takeout.

Lillian stood up and gestured toward the empty takeout boxes. "I'll deal with all this later. Go finish what you were working on." She walked over to her desk.

"Yes, Ms. White." Emma got up from the couch. Just as she reached the door, she heard Lillian curse. "Is everything all right?" Emma asked.

Lillian was sitting at her desk, hammering the keyboard on her laptop. "It's this damn laptop. It's frozen again."

"I can take a look at it if you'd like," Emma said. "I'm pretty good with computers."

"Go ahead," She pushed the laptop to the side. "It's been acting up for weeks now. I don't know what's wrong with it.

I've been meaning to have IT look at it, but I haven't had the time."

"Let me see what I can do."

Emma rounded the table and leaned down over the laptop, her arm brushing against Lillian's as she reached for the keyboard. Goosebumps sprouted on her skin. Hunched over the desk like this, she was so close to Lillian. She could feel the heat of Lillian's body, could smell the light, zesty scent of her hair.

Remembering herself Emma pressed a few keys, forcing the frozen browser window to close. "There," Emma said. "It's working now, but it's only temporary."

Lillian sighed with relief. "Thank you."

"Glad I could help. Is there anything else I can do for you, Lillian?"

Emma turned her head to look at Lillian. The other woman's gaze was fixed on Emma, a fire in her eyes that sent a shiver down Emma's neck. Then and there, Emma understood what that look was—desire barely restrained.

Emma's heart started to race. It would be the simplest thing to lean down and kiss her…

"No," Lillian said softly.

"What?" Emma asked, enthralled by Lillian's gaze.

"No." Lillian swiveled her chair away from Emma and pulled her laptop back in front of her. "There's nothing else I need from you."

Emma blinked, her trance broken. "Okay."

Her head spinning, she made her way to the door. As she left the room, Emma caught a glimpse of Lillian's pale eyes following her on the way out.

7

EMMA

"**G**ood afternoon, Lillian," Emma said.

"Emma." Lillian gave her a curt nod and dropped some files onto her desk. "Can you type these up and send them out?"

"No problem." Emma shot Lillian a smile. "Is there anything else you need?"

"No," Lillian said firmly. "That's all."

Emma watched Lillian disappear into her office. She and Lillian had barely spoken all day. Since that night the two of them worked overtime together, Lillian had been alternating between being hot and cold, distant and inviting.

It was driving Emma crazy, making her want to act up just to elicit a reaction. Emma didn't even know she was doing it at first. But it was working. Every time Emma was around Lillian, she could feel something radiating from her. It was something like a need to put Emma in her place.

And Emma wanted nothing more than to be put in her place by Lillian.

She was being reckless, but she didn't care. For once in

51

her life, she wanted to throw caution to the wind and give in to her desires.

"Hi, Emma." Bridget appeared beside her desk. "Sheryl's retirement party is in a couple of hours. Are you coming?"

"Sure." Emma had forgotten all about it. Sheryl was the office manager and had been working at AG&W since day one. Emma barely knew her. She didn't know anyone in the office other than Bridget. But her social life wasn't exactly booming, so it couldn't hurt to get to know her colleagues.

"Trust me, this party will be worth going to," Bridget said. "I heard the partners let the organizers go all out. Something about boosting staff morale. There's going to be champagne and everything."

"Okay." Emma wasn't at all surprised that her workplace had no problem providing the staff with drinks on the clock. Apparently, half of the senior lawyers drank on the job.

"Great. See you in the conference room in a few hours." Bridget wandered off to someone else's desk.

A notification popped up on Emma's monitor. It was an email from Lillian with yet more tasks for Emma to do. She seemed to be avoiding calling Emma into her office. Emma read over the email and got back to work. The next few hours passed by quickly. It was Friday, and Emma was determined to finish everything off so that she could go home after the party. Once she was done with her work, she emailed it back to Lillian and wandered down to the conference room.

Emma stopped in the doorway. The party was much classier than any work party that she'd been to. Instead of tacky balloons and a store-bought cake, there were fancy-looking canapes and red velvet cupcakes. The room was packed, no doubt because they were getting paid to stand around and drink champagne. Everyone in the office seemed to be there. Everyone except for Lillian.

Emma wasn't surprised. Lillian probably considered something like this a waste of time. But still, Emma was disappointed.

Emma spotted Bridget standing around with a group of people in the corner. She walked over to them. Bridget smiled and moved aside so that Emma could join the conversation. Monica, who worked in accounting, was speaking in hushed whispers about the firm's finances.

"Look, all I'm saying is that AG&W has seen better days. It's no secret that Gordon Sr. was using the firm like his own personal bank account. We still haven't quite recovered."

"Think they're going to start firing people?" Bridget asked.

"I don't think so." Monica finished off the last of the champagne in her glass. "Not yet, anyway."

The group was silent, no doubt processing the information they'd just heard. Although Emma had only heard the end of the conversation, she started to wonder if she had jumped onto a sinking ship. No wonder the higher-ups were throwing a party to boost morale.

Bridget broke the tension by introducing Emma to the people she hadn't met yet. It was a big office, so there were quite a few of her coworkers who she'd only seen in passing.

"Emma is Ms. White's assistant," Bridget said.

"Yikes." A woman whose name Emma had already forgotten gave her a sympathetic look. "I don't envy you."

"She's not that bad," Emma said.

"Are we talking about the same person? She once called me into her office and gave me a ten-minute lecture because I forgot to CC her on an email."

Monica chimed in. "I've been working here for five years and she hasn't even bothered to learn my name."

Bridget murmured in agreement. "I've lost track of how many of the interns she's made cry."

The sound of a spoon tapping against a champagne glass rang out through the room.

"That's Avery," Bridget told her. "I hope you like long speeches."

As the speech began, Emma's mind returned to their earlier conversation. Everyone else's perceptions of Lillian were totally different to hers. Sure, Lillian was strict and demanding. And, from overhearing several Lillian's phone calls, domineering and abrasive. But Lillian seemed to have warmed up to Emma, recent behavior aside. That had to mean something.

The speeches finished, and the group thinned until only Bridget, Monica, and Emma were left. Bridget took the opportunity to point out everyone in the room that she had juicy information on. Bridget loved to gossip, and there was a *lot* of gossip in this office. Based on what Bridget told her, half of her coworkers were sleeping with each other.

When the conversation shifted to the firm's former employees, Emma excused herself and went to grab a glass of champagne. She'd already had one, but another wouldn't hurt. She was going home soon anyway. Emma picked up a glass, then paused, an idea forming in her mind. She grabbed a second glass.

It was time to take matters into her own hands.

Emma made her way to Lillian's office and knocked on the door, her heart skittering in her chest. "Lillian?"

"Come in." Lillian was sitting behind her laptop tapping away at the keyboard. "What is it, Emma?"

"Sheryl's party is on. You're not coming?"

"I have too much work to do."

"I thought so. I brought you some champagne." Emma held up the second glass. "Have a drink with me?"

Lillian glanced up at Emma, her face unreadable. With the way that Lillian had been acting, Emma had no idea if she'd say yes or no.

"Why not?" Lillian finally said. She got up and took the glass from Emma, then took a long drink. "Christ, I needed that."

"Hard day?" Emma asked.

"It comes with the job," Lillian replied.

"Why do you do it? This job, I mean?"

Emma was surprised when Lillian hesitated. She hadn't intended for it to be a difficult question.

"I've been working my whole life to get here," Lillian said. "And I'd never be content doing anything else."

"It seems so stressful," Emma said.

"It is sometimes. But that's the price of success."

Emma tucked her hair behind her ear. "Maybe it would help if you had some fun now and then. Let your hair down a bit."

"What are you suggesting?" Lillian asked.

"That I go back out there and bring back a whole bottle of champagne." Emma didn't know where all this was

ANNA STONE

coming from. Lillian seemed to bring out a whole new side of her.

Lillian's lips twitched up in a slight smile. "That's tempting. But I don't have time. And this is already very unprofessional."

"All we're doing is sharing a drink," Emma said. "Is that really so unprofessional?"

Lillian glanced toward the door. "It is when I'm your boss and we're alone in my office."

"It doesn't matter if no one catches us." Emma sat down on the top of Lillian's desk and crossed her legs.

Sure enough, Lillian's gaze flicked down to Emma's thighs on her pristine desk. She looked back up at Emma, a battle raging behind her eyes. "You've been pushing my buttons lately," Lillian said. "I liked you better when all you ever said was 'Yes, Ms. White.' Was that obedient act a trick so I'd give you the job?"

"It worked, didn't it?" Emma smiled, her gaze fixed on Lillian. "What can I say? I really wanted to work for you."

Lillian glanced at Emma's glass. "How much champagne have you had to drink?"

"Only one glass. I'm not drunk if that's what you're asking."

"Then why are you behaving like this?"

Emma placed her glass down on the desk. "Because I've finally figured out what I want."

"And what's that?" Lillian asked.

"You."

With a single word, the wall of pretense that had stood between them came crashing down.

"This is dangerous territory," Lillian warned. Nevertheless, she took a step closer to Emma.

"I don't care," Emma replied.

Lillian leaned down toward Emma, placing her palms on the desk on either side of her. "Emma," Lillian said, her voice midway between a whisper and a growl. "Do you have any idea how infuriating you are?"

With Lillian so close to her, Emma found herself unable to speak, or move, or breathe. All she could do was stare into Lillian's ice-blue eyes as they stared back at her, blazing hot and bright.

Then Lillian kissed her.

In an instant, the rest of the world fell away, and all that Emma was aware of was Lillian's lips pressing against hers. The hungry, possessive kiss rippled through her entire body.

Lillian pulled back as if Emma's lips had stung. Slowly, Emma leaned in and kissed Lillian again, wordlessly urging her on. Lillian grabbed Emma's waist and moved in close to stand between her knees. She glided her hands down Emma's sides and grabbed Emma's hips, pulling Emma's whole body toward her. Emma threw her arms around Lillian's neck. The press of Lillian's body against hers was electrifying, the taste of her lips overpowering. Something stirred deep within her...

There was a knock on the door. Lillian tore herself away from Emma, uttering a curse. Emma barely had time to get off the desk before the door swung open. A young man with messy hair stood in the doorway.

"What do you want?" Lillian asked sharply.

"I'm from IT," the man said. "I'm here for your laptop.

You sent an email saying you've been having problems with it."

"Yes. Come in." Lillian picked up her laptop and handed it to him. "Here."

"I'll have it back to you on Monday morning."

"Good." Lillian crossed her arms.

He looked from Lillian to Emma and back to Lillian, no doubt sensing the tension in the air. "I'm going to go now." Laptop in hand, the man backed out of the room, shutting the door behind him.

Emma let out a sigh and glanced at Lillian. Before she could speak, Lillian cut her off.

"Go back to the party, Emma," Lillian said.

Emma frowned. "But—"

"Emma. This was a mistake. Just go."

Emma's heart fell. Without another word, she turned and fled out the door.

8

EMMA

*E*mma pulled up in front of her family's house. She hadn't been back home since she started at AG&W, but she was now finally getting used to her job enough that she could handle the workload without needing the entire weekend to recover. And she was feeling guilty about how long it had been since she'd checked on her family.

She got out of her car and walked down the driveway. It was good to be back. The familiar sight of the slightly overgrown lawn, strewn with bicycles, was comforting. Right now, comfort and familiarity were exactly what she needed. That kiss she'd shared with Lillian the day before, and the aftermath? It left her more confused than ever.

When Emma reached the front door, she could already hear the sounds of her brothers and sisters inside. She opened it and looked around. As usual, the house was a mess. Baskets of unfolded laundry in the hallway. Sweaters and shoes scattered about. Half-finished homework and school books stacked high on the dining table.

"Hello?" she called. "It's Emma."

A large, fluffy dog, some mix of half a dozen different breeds, came running out of the living room down the hall.

"Hey, Blue." Emma crouched down and rubbed the dog under the chin. Blue was actually white with brown spots, but blue was Margo's favorite color when they got him.

"Emma!" One of the twins barreled out in Blue's tail-wind, nearly knocking Emma over in the process.

"Hi, Jeremy." She gave him a big hug. "Where's Justin?" The two of them were usually joined at the hip.

Jeremy shrugged. "In the living room. He's no fun these days. And he's gotten really mean."

"What did he do?" Emma asked.

"He smashed my DS yesterday. Mom made him give me his, but it's not the same. It doesn't have all my saved games on it."

"I'll have a word with him." *Again*. Emma tousled his dark hair. "Where's Mom?"

"In the kitchen." Jeremy ran off back into the living room.

Emma made her way to the kitchen, Blue at her heels. She was Blue's favorite. They had adopted him for the younger kids, but she had inevitably ended up looking after him. Emma was pretty sure he only liked her because he associated her with food and walks.

Emma was accosted in the hall by her sister Lisa. "Emmaaaa! Margo won't let me use her nail polish! She keeps saying I used up all of her purple one, but it was empty when she gave it to me."

Emma pulled Lisa in for a quick hug, which was all that she would allow at that age. "I have a stash of nail polish in my room. It's in the top drawer of my dresser. You can use it whenever you like."

Lisa's face lit up. "Thank you!"

"Just don't tell Margo, okay?"

Lisa nodded, then ran off upstairs to Emma's room.

Emma finally reached the kitchen where her mom stood at the stove, stirring something that smelled delicious.

Her mother turned toward her. "Emma, I didn't hear you come in. Dinner is almost ready." She gave Emma a one-handed hug.

"Need a hand?" Emma asked.

"Sure." Her mom pointed toward the dishes of food on the counter next to her. "Take those out."

"I'll call the boys to come set the table." Emma took the food out to the dining room, calling out to the twins on the way, and then returned to the kitchen. As she watched her mom stir the pot, Emma noticed that she had bags under her eyes.

"Are you all right?" Emma asked.

"I'm fine, honey." Her mom waved a hand dismissively. "I'm a bit tired, that's all."

"Are you sure that's all?" Emma's mom had a habit of hiding how she was really feeling.

"Yes. Stop worrying about me."

"Well, I'll be around until Sunday night, so you can put your feet up a bit."

Her mom smiled. "You're an angel, Emma."

"It's no trouble."

Eventually, her mom called everyone to dinner. They all sat down and started grabbing food and haphazardly passing dishes around. Dinner was always like this here. It helped that her mom's food was amazing. Emma was a great cook. But no matter how hard she tried, her cooking was never as good as her mom's, which the kids had liked to remind Emma of every time she'd cooked for them.

Once the kids had finished serving themselves, Emma filled up her plate and dug in. She had missed this—the whole family sitting around eating and chatting over the clatter of cutlery and their mom's reminders not to talk with their mouths full. Everyone was on their best behavior for a change, even Justin. And her mom seemed happy. Maybe Emma had been worrying about her for nothing.

Half an hour later, everyone had cleaned their plates, and Emma told them to take their dishes into the kitchen. The kids did as they were told and ran off.

"Wait," their mom yelled. "Whose turn is it to do the dishes?" But the kids had already disappeared upstairs.

"Don't worry," Emma said. "I'll do them."

Emma and her mom carried the remaining dishes to the sink. She began to wash up while her mom packed away the leftovers.

"How's your job going?" Emma's mom asked.

"It's… fine," Emma replied.

"Fine? It doesn't sound fine. Is that boss of yours still giving you a hard time?"

Emma winced. "Something like that. I can manage though."

Emma's mom reached around her to grab a bowl. "I ran into Marcus out in front yesterday."

Emma scrubbed hard at whatever was caked on the casserole dish. Her mom and Marcus's mom were best friends. Both of them had been not so subtly pushing Emma and Marcus together since they were teenagers. Her mom had been so happy when Emma told her they were engaged. After Emma called the wedding off, all she said was that Emma had to do what was best for her. But Emma had caught her crying about it a week later.

"He asked about you," her mom said.

Emma dropped the casserole dish into the soap-filled sink. "Why are you telling me this, Mom?" She didn't need to be reminded of the reason she'd moved away from this place.

"I just thought you might want to know. I won't bring him up again. Although I wish I understood why things didn't work out between the two of you," she added quietly.

Emma said nothing. The truth was, she had never been able to explain it because she had never understood it herself.

At least, not until Lillian.

That kiss? It had awoken something in her, and she wanted more. She had never wanted anything this much in her life. But Emma didn't know what Lillian wanted. Lillian had kissed her, then thrown her out of her office and said it was a mistake. It was confusing, to say the least. Emma knew that she should give up on this stupid crush and move on, but she just couldn't bring herself to. And a part of her hoped that when she went into work on Monday, Lillian would take back what she said.

Emma sighed. When did her life become so complicated?

9

LILLIAN

*L*illian checked the time. Five minutes till 8 a.m. Emma would be here soon. And Lillian would have to tell her in no uncertain terms that what happened on Friday could never happen again. Lillian had spent the whole weekend wondering what the hell was wrong with her. Why had she acted so impulsively?

Lillian tapped her pen against her desk. She was lying to herself. It wasn't like she'd kissed Emma out of nowhere. They'd been dancing around each other for weeks. Lillian should have put a stop to it long ago. How far would she have let things go if they hadn't been interrupted on Friday afternoon? Was Lillian just like Gordon, unable to keep her hands off her employees?

She had to end things. It was the right thing to do. Besides, her job was at stake. After everything that had happened with Gordon, the three partners had drawn up a code of conduct. It wasn't just for show. When everything had gone down, Gordon had essentially held the firm hostage until they agreed to give Thomas his partnership. In the aftermath, Lillian and Avery wanted to make it easier to oust a partner so that nothing like that could ever happen again.

The code of conduct covered a long list of offenses, ranging from relationships with their employees to misuse of company resources. The contract was iron clad. Any "inappropriate conduct" and the other partners could push Lillian out if they chose to. Lillian doubted that Avery would actually enforce the clause for something this harmless. But Thomas Jr. wouldn't hesitate to boot her out the door if he was given the chance. He couldn't do so alone. But office politics were much too complicated for Lillian to risk it.

She was not going to lose her job over a woman.

There was a knock on Lillian's door. 8 a.m. She had been lost in thought for five whole minutes. This was getting out of hand.

"Come in, Emma," Lillian said.

"Good morning, Lillian." Emma's voice had none of its usual enthusiasm, and her eyes were filled with uncertainty.

"Sit down, please."

Emma sat down. "Is this about Friday?"

"It is." Lillian held up her hands. "I'm going to stop you before you say anything."

"But—"

"Stop. Listen. What happened on Friday was a mistake."

"No," Emma said. "It wasn't."

"Emma, you have to understand. The office has rules about this kind of thing. Partners aren't allowed to have any sort of relationship with anyone in the office. And I don't disagree with the policy." Lillian folded her hands in front of her. "I should never have taken advantage of you like that. It was utterly unprofessional. I'm sorry."

Emma actually laughed. "Do you seriously think that you took advantage of me?"

"Yes. I'm the one who is in a position of power here. I'm the one who kissed you."

"Because I practically begged you to! I wanted you to kiss me. I wanted you. I still do."

"Dammit, Emma. Listen to me. This just isn't going to happen. I'm your boss. It's against the rules. And even if I weren't, this would be a bad idea. Whatever it is that you want from me, I can't give it to you."

"Can't we—"

"That's final, Emma," Lillian said.

Emma was silent for a moment. "Okay." Her voice was so quiet that Lillian could barely hear her.

"Are you going to be all right?"

"Yes," Emma replied.

"If you'd prefer it, I can arrange a position for you elsewhere." As soon as the words left Lillian's mouth, she knew that she'd made a mistake.

"No," Emma said, shrinking in her chair. "I don't want that."

"All right. Why don't you finish drafting those letters from yesterday? I'll let you know what else I need you to do later." It was clear that neither of them wanted to be in the same room.

Emma nodded. "Right away, Ms. White." Without another word, Emma stood up and walked out the door.

Lillian rubbed at her temples with her fingertips. She did

the right thing. She may have been harsh, but she needed Emma to know how serious she was.

Before Lillian had a chance to gather her thoughts, there was another knock on her door.

"Come in," Lillian said.

A man with messy hair opened the door and inched his way toward her desk.

"What do you want?" Lillian snapped.

"Uh, your laptop? I mean, I have your laptop." He held it up before him. "I'm Stuart? From IT?"

"Right." The man who had almost caught her with Emma on Friday.

Stuart placed the laptop on her desk. "Actually, it's not your old laptop. It's a replacement. I had to hang onto yours so we can investigate. It's company policy whenever something like this happens."

"Something like what?" Lillian asked.

"A security breach. Well, it's technically it's a security breach, but I doubt it's anything serious. I found a trojan on it. It installed a keylogger and some spyware."

"In English, please."

"A trojan is similar to a computer virus," Stuart said. "It sneaks into a system like a trojan horse. Once it's in, it can control everything. The one I found on your laptop installed programs to collect information and record your keystrokes."

"Someone has hacked my computer?"

"Not in the way you think. This sort of thing is common and can be completely random. I have to remove a bunch of viruses from my grandma's old desktop PC every other week."

"Don't we have antivirus software? Shouldn't it pick up things like that?" If there was a chink in their security, she needed to know.

"It should. But this virus was new. It managed to slip past."

Lillian frowned. "Where would I have picked something like that?"

"Usually they come from spam emails or files down-loaded from shady sites. Like certain, uh, adult sites." Stuart's face turned crimson.

"I can assure you, Stuart, I'm not stupid enough to click on suspicious email attachments. And I don't spend any time on 'adult sites.'"

His face turned even redder. "I didn't think you…" He scratched his head. "That's usually how people end up with viruses like this. Unless it really was a security breach. You haven't let anyone else use your laptop, have you? Or connected any strange flash drives to it?"

"No," Lillian said.

"Huh." Stuart frowned. "We're already looking into it. But it's probably nothing."

Lillian hoped he was right. "Thank you, Stuart. You can go now."

"Right." He turned to leave, then abruptly turned back to her. "Oh, by the way, I tried to restore your files using the last automatic backup from your old laptop, but all the backups from the last seventy-two hours or so were corrupted. It was probably the virus which caused it."

"What are you saying?"

"You've lost all your work from the past three days," he said.

Lillian cursed. "And you didn't think to lead with that?"

Stuart shrugged. "Sorry."

"Just go. Unless there's anything else you've forgotten to tell me."

"No. That's all. I'll leave now."

She glared at his back as he left the room. How did this even happen? Lillian only used her laptop for work. And no one ever touched her laptop except for her. At least, as far as she knew.

All that work lost would set her back days. Some of her documents had been printed out and filed away or emailed to others. She could track them down. But her own personal research and notes existed only on her laptop.

She would have to ask Emma to track down what she could. Assuming she and Emma could still work together. Lillian sighed. It was for the best.

Then why did she feel like she'd made a huge mistake?

10

EMMA

*L*illian strode up to Emma's desk. "Come into my office, Emma."

"Right away, Ms. White," Emma replied.

She followed Lillian to her office. Things had been tense between the two of them for the past few days, for obvious reasons. Emma was trying her hardest to move on, to keep things professional between them. But every time she was around Lillian, she couldn't help but think about the way Lillian's lips felt on hers, how Lillian's touch made her whole body sing, how the scent of Lillian's skin was more intoxicating than all the champagne in the world.

Lillian sat down behind her desk. "Were there any calls for me while I was gone?"

"No, Ms. White," Emma replied.

"Did you set up those meetings like I asked?"

"Yes, Ms. White."

"Did you type up my notes from yesterday?"

"Yes," Emma said, perhaps a little too curtly. But Lillian

couldn't fault her for anything. She was doing her job. She was being the perfect employee.

"Emma," Lillian said. "This is ridiculous. I can't work with you like this."

"Have I done something wrong?" Emma asked.

"No. But we can't work together if you'll barely speak to me." For a brief moment, Lillian's expression softened. "And you're not acting like yourself."

"I'm just being professional."

"Emma, I know that you're upset with me."

"I'm not upset," Emma said, her voice rising. "I'm confused, and frustrated, and—" She took a deep breath. "You kissed me! And then you told me it was a mistake? How do you expect me to act after that? How do you expect me to feel? Every time I look at you, I can't stop thinking about how that kiss set my whole world alight."

Emma stared back at Lillian. Her jaw was set, and her eyes showed no emotion. Maybe Emma was wrong. Maybe Lillian really was as cold and unfeeling as everyone said she was, and that kiss had meant nothing to her.

"Emma," Lillian said. "You're just going to have to get over this silly infatuation. Nothing is ever going to happen between us. I'm your boss."

"I don't care that you're my boss. And this is *not* some silly infatuation." The fact that she sounded like a child throwing a tantrum was not helping her case. "You can't say that there's nothing between us. You can't say that you don't feel it too."

"I'm telling you now. There is nothing between us. And there never will be. Can you accept that?"

Emma's heart sank. *No.* "Yes," she said.

"Are you sure? Because I can make other arrangements."

"Yes. I'm sure."

"Good," Lillian said. "Now, why don't you go have your lunch break?" Without another word, Lillian opened her laptop and resumed her work.

Emma flew out of Lillian's office. She needed to collect herself. Moments later, she opened the door to Lillian's bathroom. She was so used to coming here that she hadn't given it a second thought. Or was it spite that had brought her to Lillian's private space? Lillian treated her fancy bathroom like it was part of her own house. It had Lillian's things arranged neatly around it. Right now, Emma wanted to mess up the vanity, to scatter the carefully folded hand towels next to the sink, to defy Lillian one more time.

Instead, Emma just splashed some cold water on her face and dried it with a paper towel. She rested her hands on the marble vanity and stared into the mirror. The boldness she'd shown in Lillian's office was beginning to fade. Standing before the cold, stone-faced Lillian and telling her that she couldn't stop thinking about that kiss had taken all of Emma's strength.

But now that strength was gone, and all that was left was the certain knowledge that she'd never feel Lillian's lips against hers again. And Lillian was probably going to get rid of her too. She was such an idiot for risking everything for a stupid crush that she didn't even understand herself. As she stood in front of the mirror, willing herself to keep it together, the door swung open.

Lillian walked into the bathroom, her head down, her hands tugging at the bun at the back of her head. With one quick motion, Lillian pulled her hair loose. It unraveled slowly, falling down around her shoulders. Lillian lifted her head, spotting Emma, and stopped in her tracks.

Emma's breath caught in her chest. "I was just leaving," she said.

But she couldn't move. There was something in Lillian's gaze that held her there. Something like what Emma had seen the day they had kissed. A simmering heat that threatened to boil over.

In the space of less than a second, Lillian crossed the room and backed Emma against the vanity.

"To hell with the rules." Lillian pressed her lips against Emma's.

All at once, Emma fell apart. She closed her eyes and let the unrelenting kiss resonate through her. She crushed her lips and body back against Lillian's, a soft moan rising in her chest.

With one hand entwined in Emma's hair, Lillian's other hand traveled down her side, grasping at her curves. Emma's hands roamed over Lillian's body. Lillian's neck, Lillian's chest, the dip of her waist, the swell of her hip. Although this was new to Emma, there was nothing tentative about it. Every inch of her craved Lillian.

Lillian traced her hands up to Emma's breasts, cupping them over her blouse. With deft fingers, she unbuttoned Emma's shirt. The air in the bathroom felt cool against her bare stomach and chest. Lillian reached around to unclasp Emma's bra, then pushed her hands up underneath it.

"Oh god," Emma's head lolled back as Lillian's fingers grazed her nipples. She pulled Lillian in closer.

Her lips never leaving Emma's, Lillian slid her hands down to the hem of Emma's skirt.

Emma glanced toward the door. "What if someone comes in?" Emma asked between kisses.

"No one else comes in here," Lillian said. "Do you want me to stop?"

"Don't stop. I want you so much right now."

Emma's words seemed to set off a fire within Lillian. She tugged Emma's skirt up around her waist and ran her hand down to where Emma's thighs met, tracing the wet spot that was forming on her panties.

A desperate whimper spilled from Emma's lips. Lillian tore Emma's panties down her hips and off her legs and placed them carefully on the counter next to her. She drew her fingers up the inside of Emma's thighs, her eyes filled with thirst. Emma trembled with anticipation. Lillian slipped a finger into Emma's slit and ran it up and down her folds.

Emma shuddered, her very being threatening to dissolve. She wrapped an arm around Lillian's shoulder, clinging on to her as she rolled her fingertips back and forth over Emma's clit. Her other hand slithered up to caress Emma's breasts. Emma bit back a moan.

Lillian skirted her fingers teasingly over Emma's entrance. Emma pushed herself out toward Lillian's hand. Didn't Lillian know how much Emma wanted her? Did she know how much Emma ached for her?

"God, Lillian," she whimpered. "I need you."

Lillian's breath hitched. Emma could tell that she was getting turned on. It made her want to make Lillian moan and gasp like Lillian was doing to her right now. The thought alone made her throb even more.

But all her thoughts disappeared when Lillian pushed

two fingers inside her. Emma grabbed onto Lillian's waist, her other hand splayed on the sink behind her, as Lillian's fingers curled against her sweet spot inside. The heel of her hand pushed against Emma's swollen bud over and over.

Emma gripped hard at the slippery vanity. She could feel the pleasure rising inside her. "Lillian," she warned. Emma closed her eyes as her orgasm hit her, her body quaking with the aftershocks. It was as if all the pent-up lust and tension she had been feeling toward Lillian was released through her body at once. Her cry would have echoed across the whole office if Lillian hadn't smothered it with a kiss.

Emma let out a long, slow breath. "That was..." she trailed off. She needed a minute before she could think again. Or stand. Lillian's body was the only thing holding her up.

As Emma's post-orgasm haze receded, Lillian drew back, her arms around Emma's waist. She was breathing almost as hard as Emma. She cursed quietly. "I'm late for a meeting."

"Oh." That wasn't what Emma wanted to hear right now.

Neither of them moved. Silence hung heavy in the air.

"We'll talk about this," Lillian said. "Later. I have to go."

Emma nodded.

Lillian pulled away and turned to the mirror. She washed her hands, grabbed a brush and hurriedly ran it through her hair, then began to tie it up. Emma retrieved her panties and slipped them on, then straightened up her clothes in front of the mirror. Her face was flushed, and her hair was in disarray. The thoughts in her head were even more of a mess than the rest of her.

Lillian finished securing her hair in a bun and smoothed

down her clothing. "Wait for a few minutes after I leave, okay?"

Emma nodded. "Okay."

Lillian hesitated, then cupped Emma's face in her hands and kissed her. "Later. I promise."

Without another word, Lillian left the bathroom.

11

LILLIAN

*L*illian looked at the clock: 7:57 a.m. Emma would be in any minute. Lillian couldn't believe she was back here again. Staring at the clock, waiting for Emma to arrive so they could talk about what happened between them yesterday.

Lillian had intended to talk to Emma that same afternoon. But after her meeting, she'd been called into an emergency meeting with Avery and Thomas. By the time she'd gotten out, it was late, and Emma was long gone. Lillian hated to admit it, but she'd been relieved. She'd had no idea what she intended to say to Emma. And she still didn't. Lillian hadn't meant for anything to happen between them. But when she'd walked into her bathroom and found Emma standing there, her body had acted of its own accord.

There was a knock on the door.

"Come in, Emma." Lillian shut her laptop and folded her hands in front of her. "Sit."

Emma hesitantly sat down. Silence hung in the air.

"We should talk about yesterday."

Emma crossed her arms. "Let me guess. It can't happen again?"

Lillian sighed. "You're not going to make this easy, are you?"

"No. I'm not."

"Emma," Lillian said firmly. "You don't want this."

"Why do you keep saying that?" Emma asked. "Stop treating me like I'm some stupid girl who doesn't even know my own feelings."

Emma's words were like a slap in the face. She was right. Lillian was being inconsiderate. She had been this entire time. She got up from her chair and gestured for Emma to follow her to the couch. They sat down next to each other.

"You're right," Lillian said. "I shouldn't be dismissing your feelings. I'm sorry for the way that I've handled all everything. But that doesn't change the fact that we shouldn't do this."

"No one has to find out. We can keep it a secret—"

"It doesn't matter, Emma. I can't give you what you want."

"How do you know what I want?"

Lillian paused. "I suppose I don't. What do you want?"

Emma was silent while she thought about her answer. "I don't know, exactly. But I only just figured out that I like women. And a few months ago, I was practicing my wedding vows in front of the mirror. I'm not ready to leap into something serious. But I don't want this to stop. There's something between us that I just can't ignore." She looked into Lillian's eyes, a slight smile on her face. "And judging by yesterday, neither can you."

Christ. It was that sinfully sexy smile of hers that got them into all this trouble in the first place.

"I can't believe I'm saying this." Lillian rubbed at her temples. "How about we take it slow and see what happens?"

Emma grinned. "Sure. That works for me."

"We have to be careful. Discreet. As I've said before, the firm has policies when it comes to the senior partners having inappropriate interactions with employees. And yesterday definitely counts as inappropriate."

Emma turned bright pink.

"Are you sure you're going to be able to keep this under wraps?" Lillian had picked the wrong person to have a secret affair with.

"I can. I won't tell a soul."

"And I mean it when I say we need to slow things down. Take a step back." Until now, everything between them had been a hurricane of passion and bad decisions. If they weren't careful, things could spiral out of control.

"Okay," Emma said. "But what does that mean?"

"It means taking the time to get to know each other properly. Spending time together that doesn't involve talking about filing deadlines, or me cornering you in the bathroom." Whatever this was between the two of them, Lillian wasn't one for meaningless sex.

"Does this mean you want to meet outside of work?"

Lillian hesitated. They could go to Lillian's apartment, or, better yet, a private hotel room. In a city of millions, it would be so easy for the two of them to escape somewhere that no one could find them. So easy for them to get lost together.

So easy for them to become careless.

"That's too risky," Lillian said. "There's too much of a chance that we'll be seen together. I'll figure something out."

"Okay," Emma said.

"Now, I have to go speak to Avery. I have a few tasks for you. I'll send them to you later. And one more thing."

"Yes?"

"You're going to stop trying to push my buttons all the time," Lillian said. "And stop giving me attitude. I want my obedient assistant back."

"I'll try," Emma said. "But I can't make any promises."

Lillian shook her head. "Get out of my office before I change my mind."

Lillian watched Emma practically float away. Was this all a game to her? Sometimes she wished that she had Emma's outlook on life.

Once Emma was gone, Lillian closed her eyes and sank into her chair. She didn't know why she was entertaining this silly affair. As a rule, she avoided relationships, romantic or otherwise. Yet here she was, pursuing one that couldn't be more complicated. Or risky.

Lillian got up from the couch and made her way to Avery's office. He was sitting behind his desk with the door open.

"Lillian," Avery said. "Come in."

It was always jarring to walk into Avery's office. Unlike the rest of the modern AG&W offices, it was decorated in a way that reflected Avery's old-fashioned style. It was all wood and old leather, and imposing furniture to match the heavy wooden desk he sat behind. Every inch of the walls was covered with mementos of his success. His degrees, awards, newspaper articles. Photos of him shaking hands with prominent politicians, including more than one former president.

Avery's clients probably found the overall effect reassuring. It added to his dependable image. But Lillian knew him well enough to see through it. Avery was more obsessed with status and prestige than anyone she knew. He had an ego the size of a continent.

"Good morning, Lillian." Avery placed his pen down carefully on the mahogany desktop.

"Avery." Lillian sat down in front of his desk. "You said something about a new case?"

"Yes. A colleague of mine was approached to take on a class-action suit, but his firm doesn't have the time to deal with it right now. He wants to recommend us to the client."

"Since when do we do class-action suits?"

"Since now. It's time we tried a different approach to deal with our recent issues."

Lillian crossed her legs. "So it's about our image?"

"Essentially, yes," Avery said. "It's an open and shut case. A construction company the city contracts with has been underpaying their workers. There's a long list of other violations. No overtime, no meal breaks, illegal wage deductions."

"Sounds like the public will be very sympathetic to a case like this. It'll make us look good to be supporting the little guy for once." Lillian had to admit, it was a good move strategically.

"That's it," Avery said. "You're the perfect person to take point on this case. A well-spoken woman will soften the image of the rough-edged construction workers, which will help if the case goes to trial."

The irony of her helping to soften anyone's image wasn't lost on Lillian.

"Are you interested?" Avery asked. "We need this win, Lillian. My caseload is full at the moment. And Thomas is, well… Thomas."

Lillian didn't know where she would find the time for something like this. But as always, she would manage some-how. "I'll take it. But I want free rein. I can't work on a case like this when I have to stop and request permission every time I need one of the paralegals to work overtime."

Avery nodded. "Use whatever resources you need. Within reason, that is."

Lillian frowned. "Is money going to be a problem? Are the firm's finances that bad?"

"I'm simply being cautious. We still have options. Laying off some support staff, for one."

"Layoffs? Shouldn't we at least look at pay cuts to the partners' salaries before we start firing people?"

"I had no idea you were so selfless," Avery said.

"None of us are hard up for money." Lillian had consid-erable amounts in stock and investments. She assumed Avery did too. And Thomas's family had wealth going back generations.

"We can consider it. Good luck getting Thomas to agree to that." He leaned back in his old leather chair. "At this point, it's all hypothetical. But it is worth thinking about. Pay cuts are just the beginning. If it comes to it, we'll have to consider a merger, which is a far better outcome than an outright acquisition."

"Mergers? Acquisitions? I didn't think we were at that stage yet."

"We're not," Avery said.

"Cut the crap, Avery. This is me you're talking to."

"Everything is fine. I'm just looking ahead." Avery gave her the same reassuring smile he usually saved for clients.

Things must be worse than she thought.

EMMA

*E*mma looked at the street sign above her. The cafe she was meeting Bridget at was somewhere nearby. She didn't have many friends in Chicago yet, so when Bridget offered to show her around, Emma jumped at the opportunity. She wasn't sure they had much in common; Bridget's only interests seemed to be gossip and high-end fashion. But she was nice enough.

Emma tried not to think about her family and how she had chosen not to go home to see them this weekend. The whole reason she moved away was so that she could do her own thing. But she couldn't help but feel like she was abandoning them—her mother especially.

"Emma," someone called from behind her.

She turned to see Bridget walking toward her. "Hi, Bridget."

Bridget kissed the air next to Emma's cheek. "Today is going to be so much fun," she said as they continued to the cafe. "There's a salon down the road from here that does the best pedicures. And there's a whole strip of designer boutiques just a few streets away."

Bridget continued listing off places that she planned to show Emma, most of which involved shopping. It seemed that Bridget had a very different idea of exploring the city than Emma. Shopping wasn't even on Emma's radar. But then she remembered that she had a well-paying job now. Most of her paycheck was sitting unused in her bank account. She could afford to splurge. And she could use some new clothes.

"Sounds great, Bridget," Emma said.

Bridget smiled. "We're here."

They entered a small cafe. The scent of pastries and freshly ground coffee beans filled the air. According to Bridget, the small, quaint cafe made the best pastries in the city. They ordered a variety of them, along with some coffee, and sat down.

Bridget started up again, updating Emma on the latest office gossip. Who was sleeping with whom, who had broken up with whom. Quite a lot had happened since Bridget had filled her in at the party. Emma soon found herself riveted by Bridget's scandalous stories.

"So, Emma," Bridget said. "What's the deal with Ms. White?"

Emma froze. "What do you mean?"

"You work pretty closely with her. She hasn't fired you, so she must like you." Bridget leaned in. "What did you do to get on her good side?"

Emma's heart skipped a beat. Did Bridget know something? Emma just shrugged, fearing her mouth would betray her.

"I just wish she'd let me use that executive bathroom of hers too. Is it true that sink is made of gold?"

Emma laughed. "Nope. But it's huge. It has a shower and everything. And the lighting by the mirror is amazing."

"You're so lucky. They still haven't fixed the ladies room." Bridget sighed. "What's Ms. White really like? You've got to have something juicy on her."

"Well, you know how Ms. White is. She doesn't give much away." Emma almost called her "Lillian," which no doubt would be suspicious. "You've been working at the firm for a while. You probably know more about her than me."

"Most of what I know is from before my time," Bridget said. "Apparently, she was one of those genius kids. Started college when she was sixteen and graduated from law school when she was twenty-two. She was already working at AG&W as an intern, so she got a job there right away."

Lillian started college at sixteen? Emma barely remembered what she was doing at sixteen, but she was pretty sure she was struggling to pass her English class.

Bridget continued. "She worked her way up the ladder and became a partner in her late twenties. There were a lot of rumors going around because of how young she was and how close she was to Avery. I mean, a partner picking a hot young woman as his protege? Everyone assumed they were sleeping together." Bridget paused, the way that she always did when she had something interesting to share. "But it turned out she was a lesbian all along. When I started working here, she was engaged."

"Engaged? To who?" Emma hoped that the surprise in her voice didn't give anything away.

Bridget shrugged. "I've forgotten her name. She was pretty, though. She would stop by to see Ms. White sometimes. They were engaged for years. In my opinion, if you're engaged that long but don't actually get married, there's usually a good reason."

"What happened?" Emma asked.

"I heard her fiancée dumped her. I don't blame her. The two of them were complete opposites. Ms. White's fiancée was so nice. I think she said more to me the few times we spoke than Ms. White has the whole time I've worked there. That was all years ago though."

Emma sat back pensively. At the very least, this meant that Lillian wasn't entirely emotionless. She'd been engaged. She'd been in love before.

"So," Bridget said. "Is there anyone special in your life?"

"Nope," Emma replied. "I'm totally single." It was true. She doubted whatever it was she had with Lillian counted. It was only just beginning. Besides, Emma wasn't about to tell the office gossip about it. A part of her wished she could tell Bridget. Or tell anyone. She felt like a teenager with her first crush. It was killing her to have to keep it secret.

"That's too bad. I'm sure the perfect guy is out there for you somewhere."

Emma was pretty sure at this point that a guy wasn't what she was looking for. But she wasn't quite ready to admit it out loud yet. "How about you? Do you have a boyfriend?" As the words left her mouth, she realized that she shouldn't assume that everyone she met was straight. She had never been concerned with that sort of thing until now.

"Well, there is this one guy I've been seeing for a few

weeks. He works downstairs at that real estate firm. But I don't see things going anywhere with him." Bridget picked at her croissant. "It's too bad that Tom from the office is off-limits."

"Tom? You mean Thomas Jr.?" Emma remembered the man who had ogled her in Lillian's office that day. Bridget had called him "Tom" that first morning that Emma had walked into AG&W.

"Yeah. He's totally into me. And he's pretty hot himself. But he can't act on it because of some stupid rule about not dating partners. Not that it will matter if the firm collapses."

"What? Is the firm in trouble?" Emma asked.

"Well, Monica told me that AG&W is pretty much bankrupt. We've only got a few months before we'll all be out of jobs."

"Seriously?" Emma asked.

Bridget shrugged "Probably."

Emma doubted it was quite as bad as Bridget said. She was prone to exaggeration. Still, Emma wondered how Lillian was handling the fact that her firm was on the brink of collapse.

They finished their coffee, and Bridget announced that it was time to go shopping. Bridget and Emma walked a few blocks north until they came to a street which seemed to be made up of designer clothing and shoe stores. Emma followed Bridget into the first one they came to. The shop assistant greeted Bridget by name.

"I spend a quarter of my paycheck here," Bridget explained. "Let's be real, most of my job is to sit around and look pretty. Which gives me an excuse to go crazy here every now and then."

Emma was no longer surprised by Bridget's frankness. It was becoming clear that Bridget was much more than the photo-perfect smile she put on for every client who walked into AG&W.

Bridget started strategically going through the racks one by one. Emma picked up a blouse at random and looked at the price tag. It wasn't cheap. But she could afford it now. She ran her hands over the delicate chiffon. There were some really nice clothes here.

"What do you think of this?" Bridget held up a dark red dress. It was about knee-length and extremely form-fitting. "It would be great for work."

"It's cute," Emma replied. "You should try it on."

Bridget rolled her eyes. "It's for you. Do you really think I can wear this color without looking washed out? It's perfect for your complexion." Bridget thrust it at Emma.

"I can't pull off something like that."

"Why not? You've got the figure for it. You should flaunt it more often."

Emma eyed it warily. It wasn't her usual style. But there was no harm in trying it on. "Okay."

They went around the store, Bridget grabbing items for herself and foisting others upon Emma. She was starting to feel like Bridget was using her as a dress-up doll. When clothing in their arms started to pile up, the saleswoman came over to help them.

Finally, they made their way to the luxurious dressing rooms. The first thing Emma tried on was the red dress. She had just done up the zipper when Bridget called out to her from next door.

"Well? Are you going to show me what you've got on?" Bridget asked.

"Sure." Emma slid back the curtain and stepped out of the dressing room.

Bridget was wearing a skintight sheath dress. It was very Bridget. Before Emma could comment on it, Bridget squealed. "Oh my god, you look amazing!" Bridget pulled Emma over to stand in front of the full-length mirror. "I told you it would suit you. You have to get it."

Emma turned before the mirror. The dress was as form-fitting as she had thought, but not in a skimpy way. It had a wide waistband with a small red bow at the front. Emma liked it. Her style was usually more on the pretty, girly side, mostly because she hadn't even thought about her wardrobe since she was a teenager. But this was the perfect mix of cute and professional.

"You're getting it, right?" Bridget asked.

Emma smiled. "Definitely."

They tried on the huge collection of clothes they had selected. Bridget bought almost everything she tried, which explained why the saleswoman had greeted them so warmly. Emma settled on a few pieces, including the dress. After they finished their purchases, Bridget dragged Emma to another store a few doors down.

They repeated this process over and over until Emma's feet ached. They stopped in another cafe to rest, dumping all their shopping bags at their feet. Emma basically had a whole new work wardrobe. It was much more stylish than her old one. She was glad she'd let Bridget talk her into it. She'd drew the line at heels, to Bridget's dismay. Emma didn't mind heels, but she wasn't going to wear them every day at work since she was constantly on her feet going back and forth between her desk and Lillian's office. But she bought some shiny, pointy-toed black flats, as well as a nice black dress that Emma had no occasion to wear it to, which was probably a good thing because it was far more revealing than anything she owned.

"I'm all shopped out," Emma said. "I can't take another step."

"Why do you think I left the pedicures for last?" Bridget said. "Think you can make it to the salon?"

A foot spa and massage sounded good to Emma. "I think I'll manage."

As the two of them left the cafe, Emma couldn't help but wonder what Lillian would think of her new look.

13

EMMA

*E*mma walked into the office on Monday with a spring in her step. She was wearing the red dress she had bought on the weekend and her new flats, and she'd put in a little bit of effort with her hair and makeup. It was nothing over the top, but her stylish dress seemed to call for something more than her usual last-minute look.

Emma greeted Bridget as she passed the reception desk.

"Wow," Bridget said. "You look amazing. I told you that dress was perfect for you."

Emma smiled. "Thanks, Bridget." She made her way to her desk, dropped off her things, and went to report to Lillian.

"Good morning, Lillian," Emma said, placing Lillian's coffee on her desk.

Lillian glanced at Emma, then ran her eyes up and down Emma's body, an indecipherable expression on her face.

"What is it?"

"What are you wearing?" Lillian asked.

Emma tugged her dress down self-consciously. "You don't like it?"

"Oh, I like it." Lillian leaned back in her chair, stripping Emma with her gaze. "I just don't know how I'm going to be able to get any work done with you walking around like that."

Somewhere inside Emma, longing flickered to life. The two of them hadn't even touched since that day they spoke about keeping things between them a secret. With Lillian's class-action suit, she was being run off her feet. And she had been passing on more responsibility to Emma. Lillian delegated most of the work to a handful of paralegals and junior associates that she deemed "not entirely useless," and she left it to Emma to act as a go-between and keep track of what everyone was working on. So, Lillian and Emma hadn't had the time to do anything other than work.

Apparently, Lillian was thinking the same thing. "I've found somewhere for us to sneak away to, so we can spend a little time together today."

"Where are we going?" Emma asked.

"You'll find out soon. For now, we should get to work."

The rest of the morning passed as usual. Emma tried not to get too distracted by the prospect of escaping the office with Lillian. She wondered what Lillian's definition of "taking things slow" meant. Did she mean in the physical sense? Emma certainly hoped not. Besides, that ship had already sailed.

Around midday, Lillian appeared in front of Emma's desk. "I'm going out to lunch. I'll be back in forty-five minutes."

"Okay," Emma replied. Lillian rarely went out for lunch unless it was for a business meeting.

Lillian handed Emma a file. "I need you to look over these immediately."

For a fraction of a second, Emma caught something of a suggestion in Lillian's eyes. Then Lillian turned and disappeared toward the exit.

Emma opened the folder. Sure enough, there was a sticky note on top of the stack of paper inside.

Meet me on the 41st floor in 10 minutes. Suite 223. Try to be discreet.

The forty-first floor? That was the floor beneath theirs. Emma had never been down there. For the next ten minutes, Emma sat at her desk, filled with nervous excitement. She didn't even bother trying to get any work done.

As soon as ten minutes passed, she grabbed her coat and purse and left as if she were going to lunch. She hopped in the elevator, which was thankfully empty, and caught it down to the floor below.

The entire floor seemed to be made up entirely of vacant offices, some midway through renovations. There wasn't another soul in sight. *Suite 223.* She walked down a hall and around a corner, scanning the numbers next to the doors.

There. Emma turned the handle on the door marked 223. It was unlocked, but when she opened the door Lillian was nowhere to be found. It was empty, save for various items of furniture pushed against the walls, all covered in plastic sheets. Emma wandered over to a worn-out couch and lifted the sheet covering it, creating a cloud of dust. Once it settled, she sat down and waited.

Less than a minute later, Lillian entered the room, a

paper bag in her hand and coffee in the other. "Emma. I brought us lunch."

"Thanks," Emma said. The fact that Lillian hadn't pounced on Emma the minute she walked through the door suggested she was serious about "taking things slow."

Lillian dragged a small table over to the couch, set the food on top of it, and sat down next to Emma. "We only have thirty minutes." Lillian set a thirty-minute timer her phone and placed it to the side on the table.

The timer seemed to be counting down much too fast. Lillian unpacked the paper bag, laying out an assortment of sandwiches and salads from the gourmet deli across the street.

"I know this isn't glamorous, but our options are limited," Lillian said.

"It's okay." Emma grabbed a sandwich. "What is this place?"

"AG&W leased it to use as an extra meeting room a while back, but our plans were put on hold," Lillian said. "Everyone has forgotten about it, so we can be alone here without having to worry about getting caught."

"It's definitely better than the bathroom," Emma said.

A hint of a smile crossed Lillian's face. "I wanted to take you out to lunch, but that would look suspicious."

"Why?" Emma asked. "We'd just be two people who work together, out on a lunch break."

"I don't make a habit of getting friendly with people who work under me."

"Am I the exception?"

"You are," Lillian said. "This is all very unexpected."

"It is for me too. I didn't even know I was interested in

women until now," Emma admitted. "I feel pretty stupid for not working it out sooner."

"It's not stupid. You wouldn't be the first person in their twenties to figure out that they're not straight."

"It's just that it seems so obvious now, but I've never even thought about liking women as a possibility. I've always been a romantic, and my entire life I've had this idea in my head that I'd meet my Prince Charming and he'd sweep me off my feet. But as I got older, and it didn't happen, I began to think that love and romance only existed in those old paperbacks my mom used to read." What Emma didn't say out loud was that she'd been stealing those same romance novels to read after her mom was done with them since she was twelve years old. "I grew out of the idea of a fairytale ending a long time ago. But it's taken me this long to even consider that maybe I was looking in the wrong place all along. And now I feel like I've wasted so much time."

"I wouldn't be too worried," Lillian said. "We're all going through life blind. No one has it all figured out."

"Not even you?" Emma asked.

Lillian looked out into the empty room. "Not even me. Sure, I may have my career all figured out, but I've had to make a lot of sacrifices to get here. It's meant that other areas in my life have been neglected."

"Do you regret it? Choosing to put your career first?"

"No. If I could go back, I wouldn't do anything differently. But there's no denying I've paid a heavy price for success."

"I wish I felt that sure about anything," Emma said. "I still don't know what I want to do with my life. I feel like up until now, I've been living for everyone else. I moved here to start living for me, but I don't even know how to do that yet. And I constantly feel torn between what's best for me and what's best for my family. I suppose I don't regret my past choices either, but I have no idea about the future. Sometimes I feel like I've missed out on my youth because of my family obligations, and other times I feel I haven't had any life experience. But when I think about it, I've had far more life experience than most people my age. Looking after four kids and my mom..." Emma was rambling. And she hadn't meant to bring up her mom. The complexity of her illness was more than Emma wanted to explain to Lillian. "I don't know what I'm trying to say."

"I think I understand," Lillian said. "You're trying to find a life and identity that doesn't revolve around your family."

"Something like that." Emma picked at her sandwich. "Can I ask you something?"

"Go ahead."

"You said this was unexpected for you too. Why?"

Lillian was silent for a moment. "I haven't done anything like this in a while...Had a fling, or a lover, or a relationship."

"Why not?" Emma asked.

"Like I said, I'm married to the job. I don't have much of a personal life. All my time and energy are taken up by work."

"Is that why you said you couldn't give me what I want?" Emma asked. "Because you don't have room in your life for a relationship?"

"It's not that I'm ruling it out," Lillian said. "It's just... complicated."

Emma put her hand on Lillian's. The conversation had taken a more serious turn than she had intended. "Don't worry. I meant it when I said I'm all for taking it slow. I'm not expecting anything more."

Emma leaned over and kissed Lillian gently. It was meant to be quick and sweet. But when she pulled away, Lillian drew her back in. The kiss stretched out, growing more and more ravenous. Soon, their half-eaten lunch spread was forgotten.

Emma she threw one leg over Lillian's lap and straddled her on her knees, overcome with need. Lillian seized Emma's hips and drew her in close, closing the gap between them. Their hands wandered over each other's bodies, grabbing fistfuls of fabric and caressing each other's curves.

Emma snaked her hands down and tugged the bottom of Lillian's blouse out of her waistband. She slipped her hands underneath Lillian's shirt, running them up the soft skin of Lillian's stomach, kneading Lillian's breasts over her thin bra. Lillian sank back into the couch, murmuring with bliss.

"Are we still taking it slow?" Emma teased.

"Don't you dare stop," Lillian said.

Emma didn't have to be told twice. She had wanted this since that day in the bathroom. She slid her hands back down to the waistband of Lillian's pants and fumbled with the button. Lillian shifted underneath her impatiently.

Suddenly, the timer on Lillian's phone started blaring.

Lillian uttered a curse and reached around Emma to silence it. "We should get back," Lillian said, pushing Emma away.

Emma withdrew her hands but didn't move from Lillian's lap. "Do we really have to?"

"We do," Lillian said. "We've been down here for far too long. And the last thing we need is people wondering where we are. Come on. Up." She swatted Emma on the side of her ass.

Emma sighed and got up.

Lillian stood up and tucked her blouse back into her pants. "Wait five minutes, then come back up. And remember, we're strictly business in the office from now on."

14

LILLIAN

$\mathcal{I}$t quickly became apparent to Lillian that Emma wasn't very good at keeping things "strictly business." She had no trouble remaining professional when other people were around. But as soon as they were alone, Emma would tease and tempt Lillian until she had to do something about it.

Which was why, after returning from a lunchtime meeting, Lillian found herself in her office pinning Emma to the wall with her lips for the third time that week. Emma squirmed against Lillian, her hands wandering dangerously close to the top button of Lillian's blouse.

Lillian drew back. "We have to get back to work." She had learned her lesson after their near miss the first time they kissed in her office.

Emma didn't release her grip on Lillian's shirt. "Last time I checked, you were the boss. We don't have to do anything if we don't want to." She trailed her lips down the side of Lillian's neck.

"That's enough." Lillian grabbed Emma's wrists and

pinned them to the wall beside her. "What did I say to you about being disobedient?"

"I thought you only meant when we were working."

"Then you haven't been paying attention."

Emma shot her a wicked smile. "Maybe you need to remind me? Teach me a lesson?"

"I should have known you weren't as sweet and innocent as you pretend to be," Lillian said. "I think I *will* teach you a lesson. Not right now. But soon."

"What do you mean?"

"You'll have to wait and see." Lillian released Emma's wrists. "Back to work. Now."

"Yes, Ms. White," Emma said.

Ignoring the sultry look Emma gave her, Lillian walked over to her desk. "Before you go, I need you to find me those…" Lillian froze in place. Something was off.

"What's the matter?" Emma asked.

Lillian surveyed her desk. "Did you touch anything on my desk?"

"No. I haven't been in here since you left for your lunch meeting."

"Did anyone come in here while I was gone?"

"I don't think so. But I left for ten minutes to grab something to eat. Why?"

Lillian looked around the room. "My things have been moved. On my desk, on the table there."

"How can you tell?" Emma asked. "Everything looks the same to me."

"I'm very particular about where I put things. They're not where I left them. Not exactly." It was like someone had gone through everything in her office but tried to cover their tracks. They did a good job. But Lillian wasn't fooled. "You're sure you didn't see anyone come in here?"

"I'm sure. Maybe someone was searching for a file or something."

"That must be it," Lillian said.

Emma seemed to accept her answer. But Lillian wasn't convinced. No one would go into her office without her express permission. And they wouldn't have gone through everything if they were looking for a file. First Lillian's laptop was hacked, then this? Something strange was going on.

Lillian dismissed Emma, then combed her office to see if anything was missing. The search only confirmed her fears. Although nothing had been taken, more items were out of place than she initially thought. Was someone looking for something specific? And who could it be? She could ask around, see if Bridget or anyone else had seen anything unusual. But Lillian wasn't sure what "unusual" meant. Someone from the office, sneaking around outside their department, perhaps?

Giving up, she sat down at her desk. Maybe it was all in her imagination. And right now, she had work to do.

The day only got worse from there. In the evening, she met up with Avery and Thomas Jr. The firm's finances were now far enough into the red that layoffs and pay cuts were no longer hypothetical. Avery agreed with Lillian that cuts to the partners' salaries was the better option. If they started firing staff, they might as well announce to the world that they were having financial troubles. Thomas reluctantly agreed.

By the time the meeting was over, Lillian decided that

she'd had enough for the day. And although Emma didn't know it, the two of them had plans for the night. Lillian still wasn't willing to risk seeing Emma outside the office, so she had to be creative.

Lately, Lillian had started to wonder if her refusal to meet Emma outside work really was about the risk. Perhaps it was Lillian's way of trying to keep some semblance of control over the situation by drawing a line. It wasn't working. Lillian was already thinking about crossing that line.

Lillian called Emma into her office. No more than ten seconds later, Emma appeared in front of her desk.

"Is everything all right, Lillian?"

The stress of the day must have shown on Lillian's face. "It's nothing. Just firm business."

"Oh." Emma seemed to hesitate.

"What is it?" Lillian asked.

"Well, I heard that the firm is having some financial difficulties."

Lillian rubbed at her temples. "Where did you hear that?"

"Bridget told me the other weekend," Emma admitted.

Lillian cursed. If Bridget knew, it was only a matter of time before the whole office would know. Then the news would spread quickly outside the firm to their clients and competition.

"So it's true?" Emma asked. "About the firm?"

"Yes, we're having some financial issues," Lillian replied. "But we're handling it."

Emma rounded the desk and took Lillian's hand. "What about you? How are you handling it?"

Lillian sighed. "I'll admit, it's worrying. But I didn't get this far in my career by falling apart at the first sign of trouble. I'll manage."

"I know you will," Emma said. "I'm here if you need me."

Lillian remembered the reason she'd called Emma into her office. "I have something for you." Lillian opened the bottom drawer of her desk and pulled out a small box, which she handed to Emma. "Take this home with you. Don't open it until I tell you to. I'm going to call you at 10 p.m. Understood?"

Emma grinned. "Okay."

"It's getting late. You should head home."

"Are you going home too?" Emma asked, her smile vanishing. "You've been staying late at the office a lot lately."

"Are you going to start telling me what time to go to bed too?" Lillian asked.

"I worry about you, Lillian. You need to look after yourself better."

"Fine. I'll go home in half an hour. Are you happy?"

"Yes." Emma planted a quick kiss on Lillian's lips.

By the time Lillian was heading out the door, Emma was long gone. It was a warm, quiet night, so Lillian decided to walk home. Her apartment was only a few blocks away. As she strolled down the street, she went over the events of the day in her mind. She was still on high alert from finding that her office had been searched. There was something going on, she knew it.

Lillian wondered if she should mention it to Avery. He already knew about her laptop because Stuart had informed the other partners of the potential security issue. But if she went to Avery claiming someone had been in her office and moved everything over half an inch, he would probably think she was having a breakdown and would force her to take a leave of absence.

Besides, Avery had enough to worry about right now. Lillian could tell that he felt the weight of the firm's problems more than any of them. Every day, it seemed like there were more cracks in his usually confident facade.

Lillian stopped at an intersection, glancing around impatiently as she waited for the crosswalk light to turn white. Out of the corner of her eye, she spotted a man a few feet behind her, standing among the crowd waiting to cross. He was taller and larger than average, but not so much that he stood out. His head was down so that his navy-blue baseball cap obscured his face, and his jeans and dark jacket were so generic that he seemed to blend into the background. But Lillian had seen him before. She had been seeing him everywhere.

It was almost as if he was following her.

The crosswalk light lit up, but Lillian stayed rooted in the spot, letting the crowd flow around her. The man crossed the street with everyone else and disappeared around the corner.

Lillian cursed under her breath. She'd missed the light because she was jumping at shadows. Perhaps it wasn't the same man. Or it was, and he simply lived in the same area as her. That had to be it.

But as Lillian stood there waiting for the light to turn again, she couldn't shake the feeling that someone was out to get her.

When Emma got home that night, she had a quick dinner and then hopped in the shower. She hummed to herself as she washed her hair, wondering what was in the box Lillian had given her and what their late-night phone call would entail. This whirlwind fling of theirs left Emma feeling breathless at every turn. *Lillian* left her feeling breathless at every turn.

And there was something exhilarating about letting Lillian take charge of everything. Emma had spent almost ten years being the responsible girl who always put everyone else first. Now, she wanted to be selfish. She wanted to have fun, to break the rules, to give in to her wildest desires. She wanted Lillian to sweep her off her feet and not have to think about a single thing.

Emma let the warm water wash over her. She worried about Lillian sometimes. The fact that someone had been in Lillian's office while she was at lunch seemed to get to her more than it should have. Maybe it was because of all the problems AG&W was having. Emma didn't doubt that Lillian could handle it—she was the strongest person Emma knew. But no one was invincible.

Emma finished her shower and wandered back to her bedroom. She was still drying her hair off when her phone rang. She raced to the bed where she'd tossed it and picked it up.

"Emma," Lillian said. "I hope I'm not interrupting anything."

"Nope. I just got out of the shower." Emma grabbed the box from inside her purse and sat down on the bed. "Can I open the box now?"

"Not yet," Lillian said. "For now, I want you to tell me what you're wearing."

Emma's face started to burn. So, it was one of *those* phone calls. Emma had never done anything like this before. "I'm wearing a nightie," she said.

"Describe it for me,"

"It's blue. And, uh, it has lace on it." Emma's habit of wearing pretty things, even when no one could see them, was finally paying off.

"Are you wearing anything under it?"

"Just panties." She paused. "They're lacy too."

"Good. Are you in your bedroom?"

"Yes."

"Take the nightie off. Just the nightie for now."

Emma slipped the nightie over her head. Her excitement was starting to overtake her nerves. "Done."

"Lie down on the bed," Lillian said. "Keep the box nearby."

"What's in it?" Emma asked.

"You'll find out soon."

Emma glanced at the box.

"You're thinking of opening it anyway, aren't you?" Lillian asked.

"What happens if I do?"

"Then this phone call ends. You wanted a lesson in obedience? This is it. Lie down."

Emma lay on the bed. Sure, she liked nothing more than to test Lillian's limits. But only because she wanted Lillian to push back. And when she did, it turned Emma into a pliant, obedient puddle of lust.

"Are you lying down yet?"

"Yes."

"I want you to touch yourself for me," Lillian said. "Above the waist only."

"Okay…" Slowly, Emma ran her hands up to her chest, her fingertips brushing her nipples. But she couldn't help but feel self-conscious.

"You're thinking too much," Lillian said, reading her mind. "Put the phone on speaker and place it down next to you. Close your eyes, and pretend I'm right there with you, whispering into your ear. Don't think about it. Just listen. Let me do all the work."

Emma did as she was told, placing her phone on the pillow next to her head. She closed her eyes.

"Are you ready?" Lillian asked.

"Yes," Emma replied.

"Tell me, what can you feel right now?"

Emma thought for a moment. "The bed. The sheets. The air."

"What can you smell?"

Emma breathed in deep. "My hair. It's wet, and it smells like my conditioner. Like flowers."

"And what can you hear?"

"The cars going past on the street. My neighbor's TV." Emma let all the noise fade into the background. "And you. Your voice."

"Good. Now, where were we?" Lillian asked. "I want you to keep doing what you were doing. But this time, imagine that it's me touching you."

Once again, Emma closed her eyes. She pictured Lillian in bed with her, on top of her, tracing her fingers all over Emma's bare skin. Her hands strayed back to her chest.

"You have no idea how badly I've wanted to touch you like you are now," Lillian said into her ear. "To feel every inch of your skin. To make you tremble under my fingertips."

"Yes," Emma whispered. She wanted to touch Lillian too. So far, their hurried encounters hadn't allowed for that. She wanted to see Lillian's naked form, to touch her bare skin, to taste her. All of her.

"I want you to open your legs and touch yourself over your panties. Softly."

The explicitness of Lillian's instructions only added to the illicit thrill. Emma slipped her hands between her thighs, pressing the damp fabric into her lips.

"Just like that," Lillian said, her voice soft and low. "Imagine that those hands are mine."

Emma recalled that day in the bathroom, recalled how Lillian's hands had felt, how her body had felt, how Lillian had felt inside her. Emma's nipples tightened under her fingertips. She wondered what Lillian was doing on her end of the phone. The images that filled Emma's mind only spurred her on.

Lillian spoke again. "Take off your panties."

Emma ripped them off.

"But don't touch yourself down there."

Emma groaned. "I want you so much right now."

"I know," Lillian said. "Don't stop."

Emma continued, a desperate longing whispering through her. She felt compelled to obey, enthralled by Lillian's words. Lillian continued to guide Emma, her voice reverberating through Emma's whole body. When Lillian was silent, Emma could hear her faint breaths. A low moan spilled from Emma's lips.

"It's time for you to open the box," Lillian finally said.

Emma reached across to the nightstand and grabbed the box. She removed the lid. Inside was a small, pink, silicone vibrator. It was shaped like a stretched-out egg that tapered into a long, curved tail, with tiny buttons at the end.

"Is this what I think it is?" Emma asked.

"It is," Lillian replied. "Go on. You know what to do with it."

Emma lay back down and slipped the egg end of the vibe inside her. The tiny tail curved up toward her belly button.

"Don't press any of the buttons. Remember, I'm in control tonight." Lillian said. "Now, you were playing with those lovely nipples of yours, weren't you?"

Emma's cheeks grew hot, but this time it wasn't out of self-consciousness. She obeyed Lillian's command, waiting for Lillian to give her permission to turn on the vibrator.

"Are you all warmed up?"

"Yes," Emma said.

The other end of the line fell dead silent.

"Lillian?"

Suddenly, Emma felt the vibe start up inside her. She jerked on the bed as the vibrations ripped through her.

"Was that you?" Emma hadn't touched anything.

"It was." As if to prove it, Lillian changed the setting on the vibrator, making it shoot out short, sharp pulses.

Emma gasped, her eyes rolling into the back of her head. The vibrations were so powerful for something so tiny. They felt incredible.

"Don't hold back," Lillian said in her ear. "I want to hear you. I want to hear everything."

Emma shut her eyes and nodded, forgetting that Lillian couldn't see her. Her hands gripped the sheets beneath her, the concentrated vibrations making her squirm with delight. Emma moaned with every pulse that Lillian sent her way. She wasn't usually this vocal, but the knowledge that Lillian was listening made sounds flow freely from her. As the vibrations deepened, Emma could feel her wetness soaking into the sheet beneath her.

"You can touch your clit if you'd like," Lillian said.

Without hesitation, Emma slid a hand down to her slit and strummed at her hard nub, her other hand up at her breasts. She let out a whimper as her pleasure mounted.

"Are you close?" Lillian asked in her ear.

"So close," Emma said between breaths.

Lillian turned up the vibe for a final time. Immediately, Emma was hit with an orgasm that seemed to rock the entire room around her. She cried out as she convulsed on the bed, her feet curling and her toes digging into the mattress beneath her.

Lillian didn't stop the vibrator until Emma fell silent. Emma lay back on the bed and pulled it out. Moments passed with only the sounds of Lillian's breaths filling the air. Emma wondered if Lillian had been doing the same thing she had been doing.

"Did you like that?" Lillian finally asked.

"Mm-hmm," Emma said. "I feel like I could pass out any second."

"I don't want to keep you up."

"Wait. Stay. Talk to me for a few more minutes."

"Okay," Lillian said. "What do you want to talk about?"

"Anything," Emma replied. She searched her mind and spoke the first question that came to it. "Tell me about the first girl you kissed."

Lillian chucked softly. "You really want to hear about that? And now?"

"I do. I'm curious."

"Well, the very first wasn't very exciting. It was with my best friend, in middle school. Neither of us had kissed anyone before, so we decided to try it. It was... sloppy. My friend decided that she never wanted to kiss anyone again. I agreed, until I started high school."

"What happened then?" Emma murmured.

"Sophie Adams happened. She was straight as hell, of course. But that didn't stop me from kissing her. We had a sleepover, and she stole tequila from her older sister, and one thing led to another. Like my friend from middle school, Sophie decided that kissing girls wasn't for her. Of course, I felt differently by then." Lillian paused. "Are you still there?"

Emma muttered something unintelligible and burrowed deeper into the covers.

"Goodnight, Emma," Lillian's voice said next to her. "I'll see you in the morning."

16

LILLIAN

"*E*mma," Lillian said, barely glancing at her assistant as she passed Emma's desk. "Come with me."

Emma got up and followed Lillian to her office. Lillian had arrived at work late after a morning meeting with a client. She had plenty to catch up on. But after last night, Lillian desperately wanted to pin Emma to the wall with her hips and kiss her till they both were breathless. It didn't help that Emma was wearing that sexy red dress again.

They entered Lillian's office. Lillian shut the door behind them and walked over to her desk. She pointed to the chair in front of her. "Sit."

Emma sat down and looked up at Lillian, a mischievous smile on her face.

"That dress you're wearing," Lillian said. "It's a problem."

"Oh? What's the problem with it?" Emma asked.

Lillian leaned in close to speak into Emma's ear. "The problem is that every time you wear that dress, it makes me want to tear it off you."

Lillian drew her hand down Emma's cheek. Emma

117

exhaled softly. Lillian pressed her lips to Emma's in a firm, possessive kiss.

"Did you enjoy last night?" Lillian asked

Emma nodded. "I did. I wish you were really there though."

"Believe me, so do I," Lillian said. "I have a few ideas about how we can make that happen."

"Really? Like what?"

"That would ruin the surprise." She silenced Emma's protests with a finger on her lips. "For now, it's back to work. I need a moment to myself to get organized."

"Okay." Emma kissed Lillian again.

"Go," Lillian said. "If you're good, I'll call you again tonight."

Emma smiled. "All right." She got up and left the room.

Lillian sat down behind her desk and settled in. A tall stack of files on the class-action suit sat on her desk. She picked one up from the top and flicked through it. The case was still in its early stages, so Lillian had her team collecting evidence and performing investigations, but she had to review it all herself. She didn't mind. The case was more interesting and complex than she originally thought. And it was nice to know that the work she was doing wasn't simply going to result in some rich asshole getting even richer.

A short time later, Stuart from IT came by with the helpful update that although they were still looking at her laptop, there were no signs of a larger security breach in their system. He said it was likely that Lillian had probably just picked up the virus randomly. Lillian didn't find that comforting. It didn't eliminate the possibility that someone had intentionally hacked into her computer.

Lillian pushed the thought aside and got back to work. The rest of the morning was a blur of paperwork and phone calls. Before Lillian knew it, it was 3 p.m. She had missed lunch. And she had skipped breakfast that morning, so she was running on nothing but coffee. She hadn't even noticed that she was hungry. No wonder Emma was on her case about looking after herself better.

As Lillian got up from her desk to go find something to eat, Emma burst into her office. Her face was ashen, and she was clutching her phone.

"Emma?" Lillian rushed over to her. "What's the matter?"

"It's my mom." Emma's voice quavered. "She's in the hospital. She was in a car accident. I have to go see her."

"Oh, Emma. I'm sorry. Is it serious?"

"I don't think so," Emma said. "They said she was fine. She was rear-ended and injured her leg, so she has to have surgery. But…" Emma swallowed. "When they called me, I thought it was something worse. I thought she was sick again."

"Come here." Lillian held out her arms and pulled Emma in close. She could feel Emma's heart racing against her chest. Lillian wondered what Emma meant about her mom being sick again, but it wasn't important right now.

Lillian didn't know how long she held Emma for. But when Emma pulled away, she looked a lot steadier.

"I should go," Emma said.

Lillian reached for her hands. "Are you going to be all right?"

Emma nodded.

"Are you sure? Can you drive?"

"I'll be okay," Emma said

"Let me know when you get there. And call me if there's anything I can do."

"I will." Emma slipped her hands out of Lillian's.

Lillian watched Emma leave the room. Seeing Emma like this made her chest ache. She seemed so unlike herself. Whether Emma was happy, or sad, or angry, she always wore her emotions on her sleeve. But just then, in Lillian's arms, she'd been so flat and detached. It worried Lillian. At that moment she wished for nothing more than to take all of Emma's pain away.

Late in the afternoon, Thomas strutted into Lillian's office without even bothering to knock.

"Thomas." Lillian suppressed the irritation boiling inside her. So far, she'd kept her promise to Avery to be civil with him, but she was running out of patience. "What can I do for you?"

Thomas didn't answer. Instead, he strolled over to the couch, sat down, and put his feet up on the coffee table. He was wearing a smug grin that Lillian wanted to wipe right off his face.

"I'm not in the mood for your shit, Thomas. Get your feet off my table and tell me what the hell you want."

"Jesus, relax." He removed his feet from the table.

Lillian waited. "Well?"

"I know about you and Emma, Lillian."

Lillian's heart stopped. Had they slipped up somewhere?

She could worry about that later. Right now, she would have to talk her way out of this. Fortunately, her poker face was impenetrable. "What are you talking about, Thomas?"

"You know what I'm talking about," he said.

"No, I don't."

"I saw you two in your office this afternoon. Together. You left the door open."

Shit. Emma must have forgotten to close it in her distressed state. It had been careless of Lillian not to notice. "Been lurking outside my office, have you, Thomas?" Was Thomas behind all the unusual things that had been happening to her? She wouldn't put it past him.

"I happened to be walking past. And I saw the two of you. Embracing."

"Embracing? Do you have any idea how ridiculous you sound?"

"Are you denying it?" Thomas asked.

"I'm not denying it. Emma had just gotten some upsetting news about a family member. She left early because of it. I was consoling her."

"Consoling her? We both know that you don't give a damn about anyone's feelings." Thomas sneered. "You know, it all makes sense. You two always seemed a little too cozy. The way she's always in your office. And always calling you 'Lillian.'"

"Your point?"

"You never let your subordinates call you by your first name."

"Are you serious? Allowing my assistant to call me Lillian is evidence that we have some sort of"—Lillian paused for effect—"illicit relationship?"

"It sure looks like it to me."

"You're grasping at straws, Thomas. You of all people should know better than to accuse someone like this based on a hunch."

"This isn't a courtroom. You can't get away on a technicality. And it's not a hunch. I know what I saw."

"I don't care what you think you saw. You come into my office, you accuse me of having an inappropriate relationship with my assistant, and for what? Are you really so petty that you'd try to get me fired for being nice to Emma?"

"You don't get to flout the rules under everyone's noses and get away with it." Thomas crossed his arms. "You know what? This entire conversation, you haven't denied that the two of you are involved."

Lillian knew she hadn't. She'd hoped he wouldn't notice.

"Tell me straight, Lillian," Thomas said. "Are you in a relationship with Emma?"

"No. I'm not in a relationship with Emma." The lie left a bad taste in Lillian's mouth.

Thomas scowled. "I know that you're lying."

"What are you going to do?" Lillian asked. "Tell Avery this little story you've concocted?"

Thomas shrugged. "Maybe."

"Do you really think he'll believe you?" Lillian didn't doubt that Avery would believe Lillian over Thomas. But the last thing she needed was to have to lie to him too. Or come clean and deal with the fallout.

"It doesn't matter. Eventually, you're going to slip up. And I'll be watching."

Lillian scoffed. "You're delusional."

"You know I'm right, Lillian."

"Get the hell out of my office, Thomas."

"Gladly." Thomas stood up. "You can't hide forever."

Lillian watched Thomas leave, staring daggers into his back. As he soon as he shut the door, she leaned back in her chair and closed her eyes. This wasn't good.

Almost immediately, her phone buzzed. It was a message from Emma. She had made it to the hospital. Her mom was okay. Lillian shot back a quick text. She would have to talk to Emma about all of this, but it could wait until everything with her mom settled down.

When Emma came back, the two of them would have to be a lot more careful.

17

EMMA

*E*mma shut the door to the master bedroom. Her mom had just been released from the hospital. She had some cuts and bruises, and her leg was in a cast, but otherwise, she was fine.

Emma headed down the creaky stairs. The usually chaotic house was eerily silent. The kids were at the neighbors. Emma had just called to tell them they could come home, with the caveat that they leave their mom alone to rest.

She sighed. She had been through this with her mom so many times in the past that she was struck by the same sense of hopelessness she used to feel back then. Emma had felt it the day before when the nurse had called her at work. He had opened with the words, *Your mom is in hospital,* before stating that it was because of a car accident. Her panic still hadn't quite subsided.

Before Emma knew it, she was dialing Lillian's number.

Lillian picked up. "Emma? Is everything okay? How's your mom?"

"Everything's fine. Mom's fine. We're back home now. She has to have another surgery in a few weeks, but she'll be okay."

"I'm glad she's all right. How are you?" Lillian asked.

"I'm okay, I think," Emma said. "It was hard seeing her like this. Seeing her in the hospital again."

"Emma. You know you can talk to me if you want to."

Emma sat down at the bottom of the stairs. "It's my mom. She's the real reason it was so hard for me to leave home all this time. I was worried that she wouldn't be able to cope. I don't mean because of the kids." Blue padded up to Emma and stuck his head on her lap. She stroked his fur absently. "When my dad passed, my mom got seriously depressed. Everyone said she was just grieving, and it was normal, and it would get better. But it kept getting worse and worse. After a while, it got so bad that I had to beg her to get help. When she finally did, she was in and out of the hospital for two whole years. And even when she was home she wasn't well. The medications had terrible side effects, and her depression was still there, just muted. She wasn't very functional, so I had to look after her on top of the kids. I had help. Relatives, neighbors, family friends. But at the end of the day, it was left to me to hold the family together while making sure that my mom didn't spiral into a dark place again."

"Oh Emma," Lillian said. "I'm sorry."

"She's been doing well for years now. Well enough to go back to a normal life, at least. But I knew that my moving out would be hard on her. And when I got that phone call yesterday, I thought the worst." Emma closed her eyes and leaned her head against the wall beside her. "She never went to the hospital by herself back then. I always had to talk her into it. So when I heard she was in the hospital, I thought that it was because she'd hurt herself, or..." Emma trailed off.

"No wonder you were so upset yesterday," Lillian said. "I'm so sorry that you had to go through all that."

"It's okay. I know that my mom is fine. But I stop wondering if this is all my fault for leaving her."

"Emma," Lillian said firmly. "Your mom had a car accident. It had nothing to do with you."

"I know. I just can't help but feel responsible for her. I know that it doesn't make sense."

"It does make sense. You've got a big heart, that's all."

Blue nudged Emma's hand with his nose. She had stopped petting him. She scratched him under the chin. "How are things back there?" Emma asked.

"They're fine," Lillian replied, a little too quickly.

"Is something the matter?" Emma asked.

"It's nothing you need to worry about. You should be focusing on your family right now."

"That reminds me, I need a few days off. My aunt is coming down to help in a couple of days, but I want to stay until then. Mom isn't able to do much right now."

"Take all the time you need," Lillian said.

"Thanks, Lillian. I should go. The kids will be back soon."

"No problem. Call me again if you need to."

"I will. Bye, Lillian." Emma hung up the phone.

Emma lingered at the bottom of the stairs, relishing the silence. The house would be full of noise and activity soon. Hopefully the kids wouldn't be too rowdy. She stood up and went back upstairs. Emma peered through her mom's door. She was reclining on the bed, a well-read book in her hand.

"Is that you, Emma?" her mom asked.

"Yep." Emma opened the door fully. "I'm just checking up on you. How are you feeling?"

"I'm fine. Want to keep me company until the kids get home?"

"Sure." Emma entered the room and sat down on the bed.

Her mom put down the book. "How're you holding up?"

"Me?" Emma asked. "You're the one who just had surgery."

"Minor surgery. And you didn't have to come all the way down here just for this. What about your job? Won't that boss of yours be mad?"

Emma bit back a smile. "She doesn't mind. How are you doing?"

"You asked me that already. Why are you so worried about me?"

"I'm not, I..." Emma felt all her emotions welling up again. "When they called me and told me you were in the hospital, I thought it was because..."

"Oh, honey." Emma's mom sat up on the bed. "I've told you that you don't have to worry about that anymore. I'm much better now." She paused. "Is that why you were so hesitant to move out all this time? Because you thought that leaving would make me depressed again?"

"Yes," Emma admitted.

"Emma, I'm not going to lie to you. You're my first child. Of course it's been hard to adjust to you being gone. But I'm managing." She placed her hand on Emma's. "Do you know what would make me even sadder than you leaving?"

Emma shook her head.

"Knowing that I'm holding you back."

"You haven't been holding me back," Emma said.

"I have. I've taken so much from you. This family has. You've given ten of the best years of your life to us."

"That was my choice, Mom."

"No, it wasn't. You were seventeen. You were just a kid. You didn't know what you were giving up."

"I don't regret it," Emma said. "It was hard, but I was never unhappy. I wouldn't have done anything differently if I could."

"I believe you," her mom said. "But now it's time for you to stop worrying about us and start worrying about you. Stop trying to please everyone else. Be selfish. Do what makes you happy. If not for yourself, then for me. Can you do that?"

"Yes," Emma said, a tear rolling down her cheek.

Emma's mom pulled her into a hug. "It's okay, hon."

"I'm still staying here for a few days. At least until Aunt Leah gets here."

"All right. But then I want you to go back to the city and back to your life."

Emma sniffled. "I will."

"So, tell me about your life in the city. Are you making friends? Met any cute boys?"

Emma hesitated. She wasn't sure how her mom would react to the fact that she was having a secret fling with her female boss. Her mom was pretty open-minded, but considering she'd had her heart set on Emma marrying Marcus, she might not take the news of her daughter's newly discovered sexuality well. But she was tired of keeping Lillian a secret. And Emma's mom had just told her to do what made her happy.

And Lillian made her happier than anyone else ever had.

Before Emma could say anything, she heard the front door open, then the sounds of the twins running through the hall.

"Mom!" one of them shouted.

"Quiet, Jeremy," Margo said sternly. "Mom's resting."

Emma's mom chuckled. "She's been bossing them around like that a lot lately. Reminds me of you."

Emma smiled and got up from the bed. "She's right, though. You're supposed to be resting. I'll get out of your hair."

"All right, honey. Don't forget what I said."

"Don't worry, Mom. I won't."

18

LILLIAN

*L*illian left her apartment and got into the elevator, tapping her foot impatiently. Emma was coming back today. She had only been gone for a few days, but Lillian had gotten so used to seeing Emma every day at work. Without Emma there, her warm smile lighting up the room, the monochrome office seemed even more dull, the overworked employees even more lifeless.

Of course, Lillian would have to tell Emma about the incident with Thomas. She wasn't looking forward to that conversation. But she was looking forward to telling Emma about her plan for them to spend some time together.

Lillian didn't know what was wrong with her. The fact that Thomas had caught on to their relationship should have been a wakeup call for her to put an end to things. Yet here she was, orchestrating ways for them to be together.

Was it time to think of a more permanent solution? Lillian could find Emma another job so they could openly date. All she'd have to do was put in a few phone calls. But that would mean admitting that this was more than a fling.

That would require a level of commitment that Lillian wasn't sure she could make.

Lillian left the lobby and headed toward the office. She had barely taken a dozen steps before she stopped in her tracks. Parked across the road was a nondescript, dark gray sedan with tinted windows. Lillian wouldn't have noticed it if it weren't for the fact that lately, she had been seeing that very same car everywhere. Out the front of her apartment, by the office, even at a business meeting across town. It was like that man in the blue baseball cap all over again.

Was she being paranoid? There had to be hundreds of cars that looked like that in the city. Perhaps it belonged to someone who lived in her building. Still, Lillian took note of the license plate before continuing to work.

Soon she was buried in a mountain of paperwork and forgot all about it. When 8 a.m. rolled around, there was a knock on her office door.

"Emma," Lillian said. "Shut the door."

Emma closed the door and approached Lillian's desk. "What's the matter?"

"How's your mom?" Lillian asked.

"She's fine," Emma replied. "What's going on?"

"You might want to sit down." Lillian gestured toward the chair in front of her desk. She desperately wanted to draw Emma into her arms and pull her in close. But she didn't.

"Lillian. What's wrong?"

"Relax, Emma. It's nothing to worry about," Lillian said. The desk seemed to loom between them. "But we need to be more careful from here on out."

"Why?" Emma asked. "Did something happen?"

"Thomas is getting suspicious. He doesn't have any evidence that there's anything between us. But we've been much too careless about this." Lillian folded her hands in front of her. "If we get caught, I could lose my job."

"What? When you said there were rules, I thought you just meant—I don't know—you'd get a slap on the wrist or something," Emma said. "You're a partner! You can't be fired."

"I can be fired for this," Lillian said. "I'm sure you've already heard about Gordon Sr.?"

"Yes, Bridget told me." A look of horror crossed Emma's face. "But this isn't sexual harassment."

"No, it's not. But after Gordon resigned, Avery and I drew up a binding code of conduct to make it easier for us to oust a partner if they were involved in anything 'inappropriate.' That includes having a relationship with an employee. It made sense at the time."

"I had no idea. I don't want you to lose your job. Does this mean…"

"All it means is that we need to be careful." It occurred to Lillian that if she had told Emma that she could lose her job over this when it all started, Emma might have backed off. They probably never would have gotten together. It would have saved them both a hell of a lot of trouble. But they were in too deep now.

"Do you think he'll tell anyone?" Emma asked.

"I don't know. Either way, I can't be pushed out without Avery agreeing to it, which is unlikely. Especially not without concrete evidence. Thomas doesn't have any. And we're not going to give him any."

"What does this mean for us?"

"It means we need to set some ground rules. No messages, emails, phone calls, unless they're to do with work. Nothing that leaves a trail." It was overkill. But with the odd things that had been occurring around her, Lillian wasn't taking any chances. "And we have to be strictly professional at work. No more games."

Emma nodded. "Okay."

"I'm trying to come up with a better solution. But for now? I'm going away on a business trip next week. To San Francisco." Lillian leaned forward to rest her forearms on the desk. "And you're coming with me."

Emma's face lit up. "Really?"

"Yes. You're experienced enough now that it'll be useful for me to have you with me. You can take notes in my meetings and help keep me organized. It wouldn't look unusual from the outside. And the best part? We'll be halfway across the country, where no one knows us, for two and a half days." Lillian smiled. "I can even take you on a real date, so bring something nice to wear."

"I would love that," Emma said. "I'm so happy right now that I could kiss you."

Lillian beckoned Emma with a finger. "Come here." So much for keeping things professional.

Emma rounded the desk. Lillian pulled Emma down into her lap and kissed her, soft and slow.

Emma wrapped her arms around Lillian's neck and let out a long sigh. "I missed you while I was away."

"I missed you too," Lillian said.

"Are you sure you didn't just miss having someone to boss around?" Emma asked.

"That too. But we both know I can do that from a distance."

Emma blushed, no doubt recalling that late-night phone call of theirs.

"Let's get to work." Lillian shook Emma off her lap. "And it's best for you to call me Ms. White when other people are around. Lillian is too familiar."

"Only when other people are around, Ms. White?" Emma teased.

"No games," Lillian said. But she couldn't resist swatting the back of Emma's thigh when she got up.

After kissing Lillian on the cheek, Emma visibly suppressed her excitement, then left Lillian's office. Lillian smiled to herself. If Emma was happy now, she would be even happier when she saw the hotel Lillian was taking her to. And the restaurant. Lillian was paying for it all out of her own pocket since the firm couldn't afford it any longer. It would all be worth it.

Lillian sighed. What the hell was she doing? Taking Emma on a date? Spoiling her? Promising her the world when Lillian would never be able to give it to her?

Or perhaps she could. Perhaps this time, it would be different.

19

EMMA

$\mathcal{I}$t was midmorning when Emma and Lillian arrived in San Francisco. To Emma's dismay, the flight was too short for her to really take advantage of traveling business class. Soon they were on their way to the first meeting of the day.

Emma watched the city go by out the window. "You need to take me with you on business trips more often."

"Just wait until you see the hotel," Lillian said. "I booked two rooms. But I have no intention of letting you stay in yours."

Emma smiled. "It'll be nice to not have to sneak around for once."

"Agreed. And we're going out to dinner tonight. Did you bring something nice to wear like I told you?"

Emma nodded. That black dress that she had bought on her shopping trip with Bridget was inside her suitcase on its way to the hotel.

"Good. Although it's unlikely that we'll run into anyone we know, we still have to be careful."

"So, no making out in the middle of the restaurant?" Emma asked.

"Unfortunately, no." Lillian leaned over and whispered into her ear. "But we have the whole night for that."

Heat rose under Emma's skin. That was the part of the trip she was looking forward to the most.

Lillian sat back. "Until then, it's all business. We have a packed schedule today."

Emma listened as Lillian outlined their plans, most of which were meetings. Emma was looking forward to seeing Lillian in action. The cases Lillian dealt with were almost always resolved outside the courtroom. But from what she'd overheard of Lillian's phone conversations, Emma knew that Lillian was just as commanding and relentless when it came to defending her clients outside the courtroom. And Emma found it sexy as hell.

The morning crawled by. To Emma's dismay, most of the meetings were dull and tedious, but taking notes kept her busy. Listening to Lillian discuss the details of bank regulation with a bunch of generic-looking, middle-aged men in suits almost put her to sleep.

Late in the afternoon, they came to the last meeting of the day. Lillian flicked through her notes in the car on the way there. Emma had typed up those notes herself, so she still remembered what they contained.

The case in question involved a rapidly growing tech startup that was attempting to enforce a noncompete agreement on a former employee of theirs. Lillian was representing the former employee, a young woman named Kate Waters. Kate had quit her Silicon Valley job and moved to Chicago to start her own IT security company. She had hired Lillian to look after her small company's legal needs. So, when this issue arose, Kate called on Lillian to represent her.

They arrived at their destination, a large law office that was almost identical to AG&W. It was on the top floor, and it had the exact same monochrome, modern design. There was even a pretty young receptionist with the same perfect smile as Bridget. As they entered the lobby, a young woman with short, dark hair waved nervously at Lillian from her seat in the corner.

"Kate," Lillian said, shaking her hand. "This is Emma, my legal assistant."

Kate shook Emma's hand, "Nice to meet you."

"How are you feeling about all of this?" Lillian asked.

"Good. I think." Kate gave Lillian a tight smile.

"Any second thoughts about settling? I've said it before, you have a strong case if you want to take the time to fight it."

"No. I this has gone on long enough. I just want it to be over."

"All right," Lillian said. "This will be resolved by the end of the day, Kate. And they're not going to take your company from you. I won't let that happen."

Kate smiled, much more convincingly this time. "Okay."

It was strange to see Lillian like this with a client. Reassuring and gentle while still confident and firm. Lillian's other clients wanted a cutthroat lawyer who could browbeat the opposition into submission. But Kate didn't need that. She was an anxious young woman whose entire company was at stake. This was the Lillian that Kate needed. The Lillian that Emma had slowly come to know.

As Emma listened to Lillian go over the case with Kate, she heard a passion and conviction in Lillian's voice that she rarely heard. Lillian seemed to care about this case more than most of the cases she worked on. The only other time she had seen Lillian like this was when she was working on that class-action suit.

After a few minutes, a woman came out and led them to a meeting room, where five men sat on one side of the table.

"If it isn't Lillian White," one of the men said with a smile. "It's been a while."

"Robert." Lillian shook his hand firmly, her face an expressionless mask.

Emma knew the man from Lillian's notes. Although Robert was older, his career mirrored Lillian's, and they had something of a rivalry. They had been on opposing sides of cases for years until Robert had moved to San Francisco.

Robert introduced everyone else to Lillian. Three of the men were part of Robert's team of attorneys. The fifth man, who was seated next to Robert, was David Weber, the CEO of Weber Tech, Kate's former employer. He was the only one of them not wearing a suit. No one paid any attention to Kate or Emma.

The three of them sat down, taking their places on the other side of the table. Lillian wasted no time getting started. The initial discussion seemed cordial enough, but when negotiations began, things took a sharp turn.

"Sure, we'll settle," Robert said. "We'll settle for the value of your client's company. Miss Waters was still bound by the noncompete agreement when she started it. Any profits she has made rightfully belong to us."

Emma glanced at Kate. Her face was pale.

"The noncompete agreement only applies when an employee resigns," Lillian said.

"Exactly," Robert said. "Your client resigned. You're going to have to do better than that, sweetheart."

There was a flash of anger behind Lillian's icy eyes. It quickly transformed into disdain. "What did you just call me, Robert?"

"Uh, nothing." Robert cleared his throat.

"We're all professionals here. I'd appreciate it if you behaved like one."

Robert glanced down at his notes and muttered something unintelligible.

Lillian continued. "As I was saying, my client resigned because you reduced her salary by 20 percent. That's a textbook case of constructive dismissal. By drastically altering her work conditions, you essentially fired her. Which means that the noncompete agreement is void."

"She didn't have to resign," Robert said.

"It's unreasonable to expect my client to stick around after taking a 20 percent pay cut. And you know what stands out to me?" Lillian thumbed through her notes. "Miss Waters was the only person in her entire department whose salary was cut. My client was the only woman out of twenty-six programmers. This is from a company that has a history of sexist hiring practices and has been involved in several gender discrimination suits, which is impressive for a startup that's only existed for a couple of years."

David Weber adjusted the neck of his sweater and shifted in his seat.

"That has nothing to do with the case at hand," Robert said.

"It has everything to do with this case. But let's pretend, for now, that it doesn't matter. It doesn't change the fact that your client fired Miss Waters, voiding the noncompete. In addition to that, the noncompete agreement doesn't hold water in this situation. My client started her company in a different state. All of her business is local, as is your client's. They aren't in direct competition."

"The terms of the noncompete are clear. It covers the whole country."

"Now, Robert. We both know that that won't hold up in court. Any noncompete must be reasonable. Not allowing your former employees to work in the IT industry anywhere in the entire country is not reasonable. Any judge will agree with me. Outside of California, this noncompete contract isn't worth the paper it's written on."

Robert didn't reply, but his face gave nothing away. David, on the other hand, was starting to sweat.

Lillian's voice cut through the heavy silence. "Take the settlement. We both know my client shouldn't even be offering you a cent. But none of us wants a long, drawn-out legal battle. And I assure you, if this goes to court, you'll come out of it much worse than Miss Waters."

Robert exchanged a look with David. The young CEO said something to Robert under his breath. The two whispered back and forth, too quietly for Emma or anyone else to hear. Finally, David sat back in his chair, a sullen expression on his face.

"All right," Robert said. "Let's talk numbers."

20

EMMA

*B*y the time the meeting ended, darkness had fallen over the city. As Lillian and Emma waited outside the building for their car to arrive, Emma couldn't help but wonder why both Kate and Lillian had seemed so pleased with the outcome of the meeting. The settlement that Weber Tech had accepted seemed like an unreasonably large sum of money to her.

"Why are you so happy with that settlement?" Emma asked Lillian. "Kate shouldn't have to pay anything at all. Were you bluffing when you said she would have won the case in court?"

"No," Lillian replied. "Kate really would have won. But it's a common tactic for big companies to stretch out lawsuits like this in the hope that the opposition will give up. Taking a case like that to court would have taken an immense amount of time and energy, not to mention money. It wouldn't be worth it."

"But the settlement was for so much money. Wouldn't

the amount that Kate would save by not having to pay it make up for it?"

"Probably not. Sure, if she won in court, Weber Tech would have had to pay her legal fees. But the money she would lose in terms of working hours would negate that. Not to mention all the stress. Sometimes it's just easier to settle."

Emma frowned. "That seems so unfair."

"That's the reality of the legal system," Lillian said.

Emma was mulling everything over when Robert Sharp walked out of the lobby and joined them on the sidewalk.

"Lillian," Robert said, ignoring Emma completely. "I see that you haven't changed one bit. Still the biggest bitch in the country."

"What do you want, Robert?" Lillian asked.

"I've heard rumors about your firm," he said. "Sounds like AG&W is going through some tough times."

Lillian's face remained like stone. If she was surprised that news of AG&W's troubles had reached as far as San Francisco, she didn't let it show.

"When the time comes, give me a call," Robert said. "I know we're not on the best of terms, but I'm sure I could find you a position at my firm. Consider it an olive branch." The smug expression on his face suggested otherwise.

"AG&W is doing fine," Lillian said calmly. "And even if it weren't, I would never work for you. Not if your firm was the last one left in the whole country."

A large black car pulled up in front of them. The driver exited the car and opened the back passenger-side door.

"This is us." Lillian gave Robert a curt nod. "Robert."

He flashed Lillian a smile. "Lillian. I hope to hear from you soon."

"You won't," Lillian said.

Emma and Lillian got into the car and sat in silence as it drove off. Emma looked at Lillian's face, but she couldn't tell if Lillian had been rattled by her conversation with Robert or not. Before she could ask, Lillian reached out and took her hand.

"Are you looking forward to our date?" Lillian asked.

Emma nodded. "What are we doing?"

"First we're going to dinner. Then we're going to have a drink somewhere I think you'll enjoy. After that, we'll see where the night takes us."

"That sounds nice," Emma said.

They pulled up in the front of a ritzy hotel, its grand facade lit by spotlights. They entered the building into a huge lobby that was elaborately decorated, with vaulted ceilings and a double staircase. Right in the middle was a fountain with marble statues in it. Emma tried not to gawk. Lillian didn't even glance at it. After checking in, they made their way up to their floor. The rooms were across the hall from each other.

"Our dinner reservation is for eight thirty," Lillian said. "I'll knock on your door at eight fifteen."

"Okay," Emma replied.

She swiped her card and entered her room. It turned out to be a series of rooms, all as extravagant as the lobby. Emma went through them all one by one, examining everything. The bed was huge, and the carpet was so lush that it was like walking in soft grass. The large bathroom had gold-plated fixtures and a bathtub large enough for three people.

Emma backtracked to the bedroom where her luggage was waiting. She opened her small suitcase, pulled out the black dress, and hung it up. She had just enough time for a quick shower before getting ready for dinner.

Half an hour later, Emma stood in front of the mirror in the slinky black dress. It went down to her knees but was a bit more low-cut than she was used to. But she had to admit she looked sexy in it. The woman in the mirror was a far cry from the one who had walked into AG&W all those weeks ago.

As she applied her makeup, Emma wondered why she was putting in so much effort. She saw Lillian every single day. But tonight was special—it was their first date. The two of them eating lunch on a dusty couch in an empty office didn't count.

And somehow, going on a proper date made this all seem so real. Up until now, they'd just been swept along in a tempest of passion. Emma didn't mind. But she was starting to wonder where this was all going and if she wanted more.

Emma finished with her makeup and attempted to put her hair up. After a few tries, she gave up and left it loose. Moments later, there was a knock on her door.

"Coming," Emma yelled.

She left the bathroom and made her way to the door, grabbing her purse and slipping into her heels on the way.

She opened it to Lillian standing in the doorway wearing a sky-blue cocktail dress. Her light blonde hair fell freely down her shoulders, and her lips were a luscious pink that made Emma want to kiss them. It was the first time she'd seen Lillian in anything other than business attire. She looked so different. Softer, more feminine, but still just as striking.

Lillian's eyes traveled down Emma's body. "I like this dress even more than that little red number of yours."

The intensity of Lillian's gaze made Emma's skin sizzle. "You don't look bad yourself. You have no idea how much I want to kiss you right now." She looked around. "You know, there's no one else here…"

Lillian glanced down the empty hallway, then pulled Emma in, kissing her so fiercely that it made Emma's head spin.

Emma let out a sharp breath. "Maybe we should just stay here instead of going out."

Lillian shook her head. "This is the first chance we'll get to be together without having to hide. Besides, I want to show you off."

Emma smiled. "If you insist."

"This place is incredible," Emma said for what had to be the tenth time that night. "I could get used to this."

"I'm glad you like it," Lillian said.

Lillian had taken Emma to an upscale Italian restaurant, filled with couples eating dinner by candlelight. A band in the corner played light instrumental jazz. Emma knew it was cliché, but she was a romantic at heart. So far, she'd been so caught up in how new and exciting everything between her and Lillian was that she hadn't even thought about the lack of romance in their relationship.

But as soon as they'd walked into the restaurant, Emma had realized how much she had wanted this. It was everything she could ever ask for in a date. The decadence of it all was going to her head.

Which was why it took her so long to notice that Lillian was barely there.

Emma watched Lillian finish off her third glass of wine. She looked at the glass with a furrowed brow, as if surprised that it had emptied so quickly. Was she upset about what Robert had said to her?

"Lillian? What's the matter?" Emma asked. "You're not enjoying yourself."

"No, I am," Lillian replied.

"I know that something is bothering you. Talk to me."

Lillian poured herself another glass of wine. "You'd think that after all this time, I'd be used to this."

"Is this about what Robert said after the meeting?" Emma asked.

"I couldn't care less about Robert's idiotic gloating," Lillian said. "He called me *sweetheart*. In front of our peers, our clients. Do you think he'd address a man with such disrespect in a professional setting? I don't even care that he called me a bitch. I've been called far worse. And he's right. Do you know why I'm a bitch, Emma?"

Lillian didn't give Emma a chance to respond.

"It's because of men like him. It's because of the rampant sexism in the legal profession I've had to deal with from day one. In my first week as an intern at AG&W, Gordon kept making crude remarks to me. I told him if he said anything like that again, I'd sue him for sexual harassment. Lucky for me, he thought that being threatened by a pretty blonde student less than half his age was funny." Lillian shook her head. "I was so damn naive back then. There are a lot of attorneys like him out there who would have fired me and had me blacklisted for daring to speak against them."

Emma didn't say anything. She got the impression that Lillian didn't tell this story often.

"It was a reality check for me," Lillian said. "It told me that if I wanted to be taken seriously, I would have to become the kind of person who no one would dare cross. To harden myself just so others would look past my gender, my appearance. It worked. Eventually, even Gordon had no choice but to take me seriously. But as a result, I constantly get dismissed as cold, or aggressive, or a bitch, or worse for behaving the exact same way that men are expected to behave."

Emma could see the frustration building behind Lillian's eyes, the tension holding her body taut. How long had she been holding all of this in?

"But no matter what I do, there will always be men like Robert who will never give me the respect I deserve just because I'm a woman. I've had to work twice as hard and do twice as well to get just a shred of recognition. Yet after all this time, I still get mistaken for a legal assistant or a secretary when I show up at a meeting with a male colleague, despite the fact that I own one-third of the fucking firm!"

Lillian took a few deep breaths as if trying to curtail her anger. Emma placed her hand on Lillian's across the table.

"I'm sorry," Emma said. "I had no idea it was like that for you."

"Most of the time I don't even think about it," Lillian said. "And the industry has gotten better since I started at

AG&W. But the higher you get to the top, the more pervasive the sexism and entitlement. Now and then something comes along and reminds me of that fact." Lillian sighed. "Sorry. We finally get to go on a real date, and I'm ruining the mood."

"No, you're not," Emma said.

"It doesn't matter. My client got what she wanted, and that's what's important. It's cases like these that make up for all the scumbags I've represented."

"You don't like it? Working on the kind of cases you do?"

"I don't know. It never used to bother me. But now everywhere I look there are scandals, and underhanded deals, and cover-ups. Perhaps that's why I've been trying to do more good these days."

"You do plenty of good," Emma said.

"You're sweet, Emma," Lillian leaned over and planted a brief, chaste kiss on Emma's lips.

Emma's heart fluttered in her chest, the kiss lingering.

Afterward, Lillian seemed to return to her normal self. The evening wore on, and Emma and Lillian ate, drank, and chatted about everything except for work. It felt nice to spend time together like a normal couple.

When they finished with dessert, Lillian paid the bill and announced that it was time to go get a drink.

21

LILLIAN

*W*hen Lillian and Emma got out of the cab, they were in a completely different part of town. It was the kind of shabby but trendy area that Lillian lived in back when she was a student. They walked a little way down the street until they came to a small bar with a sign above the door reading *Sappho's*. The name was a little on the nose, but they weren't exactly spoiled for choice.

Emma squinted at the sign. "What is this place?"

"You'll see," Lillian said.

As soon as they entered the bar, their ears were filled with the sound of chattering patrons and loud music. The bar was as shabby inside as it was on the outside. The room was packed, despite it being a weekday, and the heat of a hundred bodies hung in the air.

Emma looked around curiously. "Is this a lesbian bar?"

Lillian nodded. "The only one left in the city."

Lillian watched Emma drink it all in, her eyes sparkling. Couples holding hands, wrapping their arms around each other's waists, planting kisses on each other's cheeks and lips. Lillian knew what Emma was feeling. There was some-thing magical about going to a place like this for the first time. About being surrounded by other women just like her, being open and affectionate with each other. They didn't have to hide here, for any reason.

Lillian led Emma to the bar. They both ordered cocktails with silly, suggestive names, and took their drinks over to an old, tattered loveseat in the corner. Among the crowd of casually dressed women, they attracted quite a few glances in their cocktail dresses.

Lillian looked over at Emma. Her cheeks were flushed from the heat of the room, and her dark eyes were alight with excitement. Lillian leaned over and kissed her, slow and deep.

A soft hum emerged from Emma's chest. "It's nice to be able to do that without having to worry that someone is going to burst through the door."

Lillian murmured in agreement.

"I like this even better than the restaurant. Although the restaurant was nice. So was the hotel, and the flight. I'm starting to see the perks of dating someone with money to burn."

"I should have known you were only after my money," Lillian said.

"It's definitely a plus." Emma traced a line along Lillian's arm with her finger. "Where else would you take me if we got to go on real dates?"

"Anywhere you want," Lillian replied.

"Anywhere?" Emma asked.

"Yes, anywhere. Have you ever been to Naples? The food we had tonight pales in comparison to the real thing."

"Are you kidding? I've never even been out of Illinois."

"We could do all of Europe. Spend a few months there, slowly go from country to country."

"Do you really mean that?"

"I do." Lillian didn't know where all of this was coming from. Perhaps she'd had too much to drink. She should have learned her lesson by now about making promises she couldn't keep.

"I want to go to Paris," Emma said. "To the Louvre, to all the beautiful cathedrals, to the bridge where couples put up locks with their initials on them."

"The Pont des Arts? I've been there. They've cut down all the love locks a few times, but new ones keep going up."

Emma gazed wistfully out into the distance. "It just goes to show that you can't fight love."

Lillian sipped her cocktail. It was far too sweet, but she didn't mind. Emma began to pepper Lillian with questions about where else she had traveled to. They got lost in conversation, long enough to have a second drink, and a third, before they swapped out the sugary cocktails for water.

Emma's eyes locked onto something in the crowd. "Is that Kate?"

Lillian followed Emma's gaze. Sure enough, Lillian's client from that afternoon was standing by the bar, a thin woman with deep brown skin by her side. Lillian knew Kate was queer, but she wasn't expecting to run into her here.

Almost immediately, Kate caught her eye. She waved and walked over to them, the other woman in tow.

"Lillian? I barely recognized you," Kate said. "And Emma, wasn't it?"

Emma nodded. "Hi."

"This is Jo, my girlfriend. I dragged her along to San Francisco with me."

Jo smiled. "Nice to meet you."

There was a moment of silence as Kate looked from Emma to Lillian. "I didn't realize that you two were a couple," she said.

The cat was out of the bag now. "We're dating," Lillian said. "But we're not supposed to be. Workplace rules and all."

"Your secret is safe with us," Kate said. "Trust me, we know what it's like to have to keep a relationship secret."

"Where my family comes from, being gay isn't even an option," Jo explained. "I spent the first few months of our relationship in the closet. But those days are over. It's such a relief." She pecked Kate on the cheek. "Don't worry, we won't tell."

Lillian felt a pang of guilt. She knew what it was like to have to hide who she loved because of prejudice and bigotry. Hell, everyone in the bar knew what that was like. And here she was, keeping her relationship with Emma secret for selfish, trivial reasons. Suddenly, all the sneaking around and lying seemed so foolish.

Lillian had to face the truth. She was using the fact that their relationship was forbidden to avoid confronting the real issue that was holding her back.

"Thank you," Lillian said. "We really appreciate it."

"We should be thanking you," Jo said. "You have no idea

how grateful we are that everything has been resolved. This case has been eating both of us up."

"I was just doing my job," Lillian said.

"Well, I'm relieved that we can finally move on with our lives," Kate said. "We'll leave you two to it. Thanks again, Lillian."

The two of them disappeared into the crowd.

"She's right, you know," Emma said. "You did well today. And for the record, you were amazing in there." Emma lowered her voice. "It was kind of hot."

Lillian smiled. "How about we move onto the next part of the date?"

"What's that?" Emma asked.

Lillian leaned in closer. "It's the part where I take you back to my hotel room and we spend the rest of the night making up for lost time." She slid her hand up Emma's thigh.

Emma's lips parted slightly, letting out a rush of warm air that tickled Lillian's skin.

"Unless you'd rather stay and finish your drink?" Lillian asked.

Emma picked up her glass and downed the last of her half-drunk cocktail. "All done."

"Let's get out of here."

22

EMMA

*T*he cab ride back to the hotel seemed to take forever. Emma and Lillian sat in the back seat, unable to keep their hands off each other. The cab driver gave them a disapproving look when they got out. It changed once he saw how generously Lillian tipped him.

Once they reached their floor, Lillian dragged Emma into her room. As soon as the door was shut, she pressed Emma up against the wall in a desperate, demanding kiss. Lips still locked, they made their way to the bedroom, leaving a trail of heels, purses, and coats in their wake. They collapsed onto the bed, limbs tangled together, Lillian on top of Emma. Lillian wrested Emma's dress over her head, then pulled off her own, dropping it on the ground.

Emma watched Lillian above her, desire radiating between them. This would be the first time they would see each other naked and exposed. The first time they would be able to touch each other without having to hastily force aside layers of clothing. The first time they could freely explore each other's bodies without fear of discovery.

157

Lillian reached around behind her back again and unclipped her bra, her breasts springing free as she slipped it from her shoulders. Her dark nipples were two tiny peaks on her soft, inviting breasts.

"I've wanted this for so long," Emma whispered.

Lillian's response was a ravenous kiss that sent a bolt of lust through Emma. Lillian unhooked the clasp of Emma's bra and tore it from her body. Immediately, Lillian's lips were on hers again, and Lillian's body was on hers, her bare breasts pushing against Emma's. Emma ran her hands over Lillian's skin. Who knew that someone so cold and hard as Lillian could feel so warm and supple?

Lillian broke away and lay down on her side next to Emma. "I want to try something with you," she said, her hand grazing Emma's cheek.

"What is it?" Impatience and curiosity battled within Emma. She craved Lillian with her entire being, but she wanted to know what Lillian had in store for her.

Lillian got up from the bed and went over to her suitcase, tying her hair up into a ponytail as she walked. Emma stared shamelessly at Lillian's lithe figure as she rifled around in her bag. Lillian pulled out a single sheer thigh-high stocking.

"What are you going to do with that?" Emma asked.

"I have a few ideas." Lillian stretched the stocking out taut with her hands as far as it could go.

It almost looked like a rope.

Oh. "Are you going to tie me up?" Emma asked.

Lillian climbed back onto the bed. "You're not very good at keeping your hands to yourself." She swept the soft stocking along Emma's side, from the swell of her hip to the bow of her neck. "I want to give you all the attention you deserve. And I can't do that with your distracting hands all over me. What do you say?"

Emma nodded, her heart racing. "Okay. Do it."

Lillian pushed Emma's shoulder down so she was lying on her back. "If you change your mind, tell me to stop."

"Okay." She doubted she was going to stop Lillian. Everything about this was making Emma even hotter.

"Your hands," Lillian commanded.

Emma lifted her arms up in the air, wrists together. She had never done anything like this before. Lillian wrapped the stocking around them in a complicated knot, which made Emma wonder if *Lillian* had done this before. Once she was finished, Emma's wrists were bound tightly enough that she couldn't move them, but were just loose enough to be comfortable.

Lillian took Emma's hands and pushed them up above her head, pinning them to the pillow. "I want you to keep your hands above your head."

"What happens if I don't?" Emma asked.

"Try it and find out. But I don't think you will."

Lillian was right. Emma loved to push Lillian's buttons. She loved to see how far she could go. But just like with their naughty phone call, whenever she had Lillian's undivided attention, she wanted nothing more than to yield to her.

"Made up your mind yet?" Lillian asked.

Emma nodded.

"Are you going to keep your hands above your head?"

"Yes," Emma said.

Lillian reached down and drew Emma's panties from

her legs. "Close your eyes."

Emma shut her eyes and waited, her body begging for Lillian's touch.

At first, there was nothing. Then Lillian's lips were on hers, first soft and slow, then hungry and firm. Lillian tilted Emma's chin to the side and kissed down the side of her throat. Her warm breath tickled Emma's skin.

"God, you're exquisite," Lillian said, her voice dropping to a whisper. "Your body, your skin, your everything. You have no idea what you do to me. You have no idea how much you make me want you."

A shiver rolled down the entire length of Emma's skin. She needed to feel Lillian's body against hers, Lillian's lips all over her, Lillian's fingers between her thighs, soothing the ache inside...

"Careful," Lillian's voice rang out from above her.

Emma opened her eyes. Her hands had floated up of their own accord, but they were still above her head. She put them down flat on the bed and tried to look contrite.

"Just close your eyes," Lillian said.

Emma did as she was told. Something about having her wrists bound made her pliant and obedient. She was barely restrained, but without her hands, she might as well be wearing a straitjacket.

"Now, where was I?" Lillian knelt over Emma again, feathering her lips against Emma's neck. She drew her fingers along Emma's skin with an almost reverent touch. "I'm going to take my time with you. I'm going to explore every inch of you. I'm going to make you feel like your body is the center of everything, like nothing exists outside the two of us."

Emma quivered, her skin tingling under Lillian's fingertips. Lillian slid her hands up to Emma's chest, outlining the contours of her breasts, then rolled Emma's nipples in her fingers, eliciting a fevered gasp. She leaned down and took Emma's nipple into her mouth, circling it with her warm tongue. Lillian did so again, this time with the lightest pressure of teeth. Emma thrashed and moaned, her cries echoing through the still room. But it didn't matter. It was just the two of them alone.

Emma's need grew as Lillian tormented her, lavishing attention on her bound body. The muscles in her arms tightened as Emma struggled to hold her hands in place. It was taking all her willpower not to bring them down to touch Lillian, to guide her to where Emma needed her the most.

Just when she thought she couldn't take it any longer, Lillian's lips trailed down her stomach, past her bellybutton. Emma spread her legs out wide, throbbing with anticipation.

But still, Lillian took her time. She licked her way up Emma's folds, her tongue burning like a brand. Lillian settled on Emma's clit and wrapped her lips around it. Emma clenched her fists above her head, the fire in her core blazing red-hot. Lillian braced her arms around Emma's thighs, diving in deeper.

Emma's awareness shrank down to that pinpoint at the peak of her thighs. With one final swirl of Lillian's tongue, Emma cried out, pleasure exploding through her entire body.

When Emma came back to herself, she found Lillian's

mouth on hers, stealing her breath. She could taste herself on Lillian's tongue.

Emma brought her bound hands down and traced them along Lillian's stomach. "Can you untie me now?"

Lillian exhaled slowly as Emma's hands slid further down. She grabbed Emma's wrists and untied the stocking.

Emma pounced on Lillian, stripping her panties from her hips and tossing them across the room. Her hands sought out Lillian's hips, her breasts, her ass cheeks, all the parts of her that Emma had dreamed about touching. She kissed Lillian all over, breathing in the scent of her hair and tasting the salt on her skin.

Lillian shifted her body on the bed so that she was half sitting, half lying against the pillows. Emma nudged Lillian's legs open and knelt between them, then sent a questing hand down Lillian's stomach. Lillian rose slightly, offering herself to Emma.

Emma slid her hand down further and slid a finger between Lillian's lips. "You're so wet," she exclaimed. It was the first time Emma had touched Lillian like this, the first time she'd felt another woman's arousal. It was unexpected in the best possible way.

"That's what you do to me," Lillian said, her voice dripping with desire. "Don't stop."

Emma ran her fingers up and down Lillian's warm, velvety folds. When her hand grazed Lillian's hidden bud, Lillian let out a shallow, panting breath. Emma drew her fingertip up to trace small, tight circles around it.

Lillian closed her eyes. "Yes, like that." She reached out for Emma, her hands cradling the flesh of Emma's ass cheeks.

Emma continued. She hadn't done this before, but Lillian's body told Emma exactly what to do. Her gasps, her cries, the tremors that went through her when Emma touched her this way or that way. It was all the instruction Emma needed. And the knowledge that she was causing Lillian to lose control like this was intoxicating. She ran her fingers down to Lillian's entrance.

"Oh yes," Lillian said, her head falling back.

Emma slid a finger inside. It slipped in easily. She added another finger, then, after some hesitation, another, delving deep. Lillian let out a moan. Emma slid her thumb up, rolling it over Lillian's swollen nub.

"Faster," Lillian said.

Emma moved her body faster, her fingers thrusting and curling, and her thumb strumming. Lillian's hips rose up to meet her over and over. Her moans built until her hands tightened around Emma's hips, and her whole body began to shake. Lillian arched up on the bed, her mouth open wide in a silent scream, her walls clenching around Emma's fingers. Emma didn't stop until Lillian fell back onto the bed.

Lillian groaned and pulled Emma into her. "Christ, Emma. What are you doing to me?"

Emma wasn't sure if Lillian was talking about the last hour or something else. So she simply lay there, her head buried in the crook of Lillian's neck, until Lillian kissed her again, reigniting the fire inside her.

"Mmph." Emma pushed Lillian away halfheartedly. "If you keep going, we're going to have to do that all again."

"We have the whole night," Lillian said. "I'm nowhere near done with you yet."

23

LILLIAN

*L*illian glanced over at Emma. Her eyes were closed, and her skin was glowing. The two of them had spent the last few hours "making up for lost time" until both of them were spent.

Emma shifted on the bed, resting her head on Lillian's shoulder. "I've changed my mind," Emma said. "I don't want you to take me to Paris. All I want is to lie in bed with you all day and cuddle up and watch movies."

Lillian smiled. "That does sound nice."

"I should warn you, I have terrible taste in movies."

"Oh? What's your favorite movie?"

"It's probably a tie between *Gone with the Wind* and *Titanic*."

"You really are a romantic," Lillian said.

"Don't say I didn't warn you."

"Have you ever watched *Carol*?"

Emma shook her head.

"It's a beautiful movie about a relationship between two women in the 1950s."

Emma brought a hand up to trace Lillian's collarbone. "I don't think I've ever watched a movie about two women falling in love."

"There are lots of them out there," Lillian said. "I can recommend some."

"Or we could watch them together."

Lillian ran her fingers through Emma's hair. "One day."

"I didn't know you liked romance movies," Emma said.

"I like good movies," Lillian replied. "Some of them happen to contain romance."

Emma kissed Lillian on the cheek. "Don't worry, I won't tell anyone that you're really a big softie."

"Even if you did, no one would believe you."

Emma sighed contentedly. "Tonight was nice. Getting to do all those normal couple things. Going on a date. Making out at a bar."

Lillian murmured in agreement.

"You know, seeing all those couples made me realize something. I want what they have. I want a real relationship. I don't care if we have to hide it. But I want to be your girlfriend."

"I want that too, but…" Lillian trailed off. Uncertainty wasn't a feeling she was used to having. "I don't know if it's a good idea."

"Lillian." Emma propped herself up on her side. "I know that this is about more than breaking office rules. If you cared about that, you wouldn't be in bed with me right now."

Lillian closed her eyes, then opened them again. "You're right. But I've already told you my reasons."

"What, that you're married to the job?" Emma asked. "That's the stupidest excuse I've ever heard."

Lillian bristled. She wasn't in the habit of letting anyone speak to her like that. It suddenly struck her that this was what it felt like to be on the receiving end of one of Lillian's tirades.

"I get it," Emma continued. "Relationships are hard, especially when you have a job like yours. You work eighty-hour weeks, you practically live at the office, you're always working on some big case. But that doesn't mean you can't find happiness in other parts of your life."

"It's not that simple," Lillian said.

"It is if you want it to be. You're the one in control of your life. You can make the choice to have a relationship. At the very least you can make the choice to try!"

"Dammit, Emma! Sometimes wanting something just isn't enough. Sometimes trying isn't enough. Sometimes even love isn't enough!"

The room fell silent. Lillian hadn't meant to lose it like that.

"Is this about your ex-fiancée?" Emma asked.

Lillian froze. "How do you know about her?"

"Bridget told me. But she didn't tell me the details."

"Of course Bridget told you. It's not just about my ex-fiancée, but…" Lillian couldn't even remember the last time she'd spoken about her. "Her name was Meredith. We met just before I became a partner at AG&W. A few years into the relationship, I proposed to her. She turned me down. She was a free spirit who lived for adventure. Meredith dreamed of leaving the city behind and traveling the country, the whole world. As in love as we were, Meredith wasn't sure if she could marry someone who worked as much as I did. So I told her I would change. I cut down my hours and stopped working on weekends. And things improved. A year later, I asked her to marry me again. This time, she said yes.

"Everything was good between us for a while. But eventually, I began to slip into old habits. I didn't even notice it at the time. Meredith never said anything. But a week before the wedding, she told me that she couldn't go through with it. She said that she loved me, but she knew in her heart that she would always be second to my career. I asked her for another chance. She told me she would stay if I quit my job at AG&W. But I just couldn't do it; couldn't give up everything I worked so hard for. So, she left me. All because I valued my career more than our relationship."

Lillian glanced at Emma. If the fact that Lillian had chosen her career over love bothered Emma, she didn't show it. Instead, her eyes were filled with sympathy.

"It wasn't just Meredith. All my relationships, they never work out for the same reason. The other person always ends up wanting more from me. More time, more attention, more love. And I can't give it to them. I care about you, Emma. I want nothing more than for us to be together. But I don't want to disappoint you. I don't want to hurt you. You deserve someone who can give you that fairytale ending you've always wanted."

"But I don't want someone else," Emma said. "I want you. And I know how much your career means to you. I'd never ask you to change. If it becomes an issue down the line, we'll figure it out. We'll get through it." Emma reached out and took Lillian's hand. "You won't disappoint me, Lillian. I know you won't."

The sincerity in Emma's eyes stirred something in Lillian. Emma truly believed every word that she was saying, truly believe that things could work out for them. Lillian wanted to believe it too. She wanted to believe that this time would be different.

"You can't live your entire life in fear of something that might not even happen," Emma said. "I want to give this a try. I want to give *us* a try."

Emma was right. Lillian had let her career dictate her life for too long.

Not anymore.

"Okay," Lillian said. "I want you to be my girlfriend. And I want to be yours."

Emma smiled. "I would like that."

A warm feeling washed over Lillian's body. But the conversation wasn't over. There was still another step they had to take if they were really going to be together. "What do you think about me finding you another job? We can't hide our relationship forever."

"I don't mind leaving AG&W," Emma said. "But I'd rather find a job on my own. I don't want to take advantage of my relationship with you."

"You wouldn't be," Lillian said. "You have enough experience now that you're a competent legal assistant in your own right. Any firm would be lucky to have you. You were trained by me after all."

"Okay," Emma said. "I do like working with you, though. I'll miss it when I leave."

"I like working with you too. But it'll be for the best."

"I know." Emma snuggled into Lillian again and closed her eyes.

Lillian put her arm around Emma and held her close. Soon they would have to go back to the real world. Back to the office, full of secrets and scandals. Back to pretending they were nothing more than a boss and her employee. Back to hiding what they felt for each other.

But for now, Lillian could pretend that she didn't have a care in the world.

24

EMMA

"I'm coming up there in ten minutes!" Emma yelled up the stairs. "If anyone is still awake, I'm taking away your phone."

"You're not Mom," one of the twins shouted. Emma was pretty sure it was Justin because Jeremy never gave her attitude. "You can't do that."

"I changed your diapers for a year. That means I can do whatever I want."

"Fine, I'm going." He stomped to his room and slammed the door.

Emma waited at the bottom of the stairs until she couldn't hear any more noise coming from above. She shook her head. She had missed her family so much when she first moved out. Now, after spending an hour trying to get four teenagers to go to bed, she wasn't so sure.

She made her way down the hall. It was the first time she'd been back to her family home since her mom's car accident over a month ago. Emma had taken her mom's words about not worrying about her and the kids to heart.

It was hard at first. She had to stop herself from calling her mom every couple of days to make sure that everything was okay. But it had gotten easier with time.

Her mom was due to have her second surgery tomorrow. This surgery required her to stay in the hospital for a couple of days afterward, so Emma had come down to help until her aunt took over in a few days' time.

Emma reached the living room and sat on the couch next to her mom. Blue jumped up onto the couch between them, set his head on Emma's lap, and immediately started to doze. She stroked his fur. His brown spots were speckled with gray, even more so than last time she had been here.

Emma's mom shifted in her seat, wincing.

"Is your leg bothering you?" Emma asked.

"A little," her mom replied. "But tomorrow will help with that." She repositioned her leg. "How was your trip to San Francisco?"

"Good. Mostly work though."

"Did you get to see much of the city?"

"A little bit."

It had been a couple of weeks since Emma and Lillian got back from San Francisco. The second night of their trip had gone much the same as the first one, except that when Emma's suggested they stay in for the evening, Lillian agreed.

As soon as they arrived back home, Lillian put in a few calls to find Emma another job. It didn't take long until she had an offer. She gave her notice at AG&W and was starting the new job in two weeks. They both agreed that the best course of action was to continue to work together and keep their relationship under wraps until then.

But now that Emma and Lillian had gotten to experience what being together freely was really like, going back into hiding was almost painful. All Emma wanted was to walk down the street holding Lillian's hand, to kiss her and not care if anyone saw them, to tell the whole world that they were together.

Emma glanced at her mom. It felt strange keeping something like this from her. Emma had no idea how she would react to the news that Emma was dating a woman, but she had to tell someone. She didn't have to tell her mom all the details. Just the important parts.

"I've been seeing someone," Emma said. "For a while now, actually."

"That's great," her mom replied. "Who is he?"

"Someone I work with. And she's not a he. Her name is Lillian. She's my girlfriend." It was the first time she'd called Lillian her girlfriend out loud.

"Huh." Her mom paused. "Does she make you happy?"

Emma smiled. "She does."

"Then I'm happy for you."

They sat in silence until her mom started to chuckle.

"What is it?" Emma asked.

"When you were a kid, you used to hold these elaborate weddings between your Barbie dolls. You made me and your dad come watch and everything. It all makes sense now."

Emma rolled her eyes. "I was just being a kid." She only had vague memories of that. Apparently, she'd been a romantic for even longer than she remembered.

"Does this mean you're a lesbian now? You could be bisexual, you know. Have you heard of bisexuals?"

"Mom, I know what bisexual means." Emma sighed. "I'm not bisexual. At least I don't think I am. And I'm not a lesbian now. I think I've always been attracted to women, I just... it's complicated."

"Is that why things didn't work out with Marcus?"

"I think so." That was one loose end she'd have to tie up. Emma still cared about him. And part of why he'd been so devastated by the breakup was because neither of them understood her reasons. Telling Marcus that it was because she wasn't interested in men might help him move on.

"Huh. I guess that makes sense." Her mom sat back in her chair. "Are you still going to get married one day?"

"Of course I am. Why would that change?"

Her mom smiled. "I guess you are still the same Emma."

For a split second, Emma wondered if Lillian ever wanted to get married. Then she realized how crazy it was to think about all of that since they'd only been officially a couple for a few weeks.

"Well, I'm glad that you've found someone, honey. I meant what I said to you last time you were here. About living for yourself. I'm happy to see that you've started doing that."

"Thanks, Mom." Emma finally felt confident that her life was going in the right direction. She had found a balance between her own desires and her family. She and Lillian were a couple now. And she saw them having a future together.

All she needed was to make it through the next two weeks.

25

LILLIAN

"Chelsea." Lillian sat down across from Chelsea at their usual table at their usual restaurant. She and Chelsea were long overdue for a catch-up.

"Hi, Lillian," Chelsea said. "How was San Francisco?"

"It was good," Lillian replied.

"Good? You usually describe your business trips as 'painfully dull.'"

"What can I say? San Francisco is a lovely city." Lillian changed the subject. "How's married life treating you?"

"It's nice. I didn't think a ceremony and a piece of paper would change anything between us. But it has. Everything just feels so much more intimate." Chelsea smiled. "Maybe it's all in my head."

Every time Chelsea spoke about her now husband, Lillian could hear the affection in her words. A love like theirs had always seemed impossible to Lillian. But she was starting to understand just how possible it was.

Chelsea frowned. "Something is definitely going on. You're acting strangely."

Lillian was saved when the waiter came by to take their orders. She ordered the same thing as always, along with some sparkling water.

As soon as they were left alone, Chelsea started up again. "Now, where were we? You were about to tell me why you're staring wistfully off into the distance?"

"It's a long story," Lillian replied

"Wait." Chelsea leaned forward. "You've met someone, haven't you?"

Lillian hesitated. It wasn't like Chelsea was going to tell anyone. "Yes, I have."

"Seriously?" Chelsea's face lit up. "Who is this woman who has melted the Ice Queen's heart?"

Lillian was beginning to regret ever telling Chelsea about that nickname. "Her name is Emma. Do you remember that new legal assistant I mentioned?"

Chelsea tilted her head to the side. "Really?"

"Yes, really. I know that I said I'd never go there. But I did. And once everything started, I didn't want to stop. I took her with me to San Francisco, and now she's my girlfriend."

"Wow," Chelsea said. "Doesn't your firm have a policy about partners dating their employees?"

Lillian nodded. "We've been keeping it a secret."

"You're willing to risk your job over this woman?"

"I don't know. To be honest, the more I think about it, the less I care about the effect it could have on my job. I'm tired, Chelsea. Tired of defending corporate scumbags and helping the absurdly wealthy become even wealthier. Tired of my career dominating my life. I've been sick of it all for a while now. I just didn't realize it until Emma came along and reminded me that there's so much more to life."

"This Emma of yours must be pretty special," Chelsea said.

"She is." Lillian sighed. "I don't want to hide our relationship anymore. I've found her a new job, but until then, we're going to have to keep everything under wraps."

"You'll get through it." Chelsea smiled reassuringly. "I'm happy for you, Lillian."

"Thanks, Chelsea."

"So, when do I get to meet Emma? You two should come over to dinner sometime."

"Sure," Lillian said. The idea of having to sit through dinner with Chelsea and her husband behaving all lovey-dovey would normally have bored her. But for some reason, it sounded nice. Maybe Emma's romantic notions were rubbing off on her.

The waiter arrived with their food. Lillian noticed too late that he had forgotten her sparkling water. She turned in her chair and scanned the room for him.

Lillian froze. Sitting by himself at a table in the corner was a familiar-looking man. He wasn't wearing his blue baseball cap, and he had a dark blazer on instead of a jacket. But his build, and the way he held himself, told Lillian that it was the same man she had been seeing everywhere.

"Chelsea," Lillian said. "Try not to stare, but there's a man at the table in the corner behind me." She shifted in her seat so that Chelsea could get a better look. "Do you know him?"

The restaurant was almost exclusively patronized by lawyers and businesspeople, most of whom were regulars like Lillian and Chelsea. Between the two of them, they knew almost everyone in the room.

Chelsea glanced at the man, then returned her gaze to Lillian. "No, I've never seen him before. Why?"

"It's nothing," Lillian said. "Forget that I said anything."

"All right," Chelsea replied.

Lunch passed by quickly. It wasn't long before they both had to go back to work. Before they left the restaurant, Lillian looked over at the table in the corner.

The man was gone.

By the time Lillian got home from work, it was dark. She unlocked her door and entered her apartment, flipping through her mail as she walked. It was mostly bills. She placed it on the table in the hall, then went into the living room and flicked on the light.

She stopped in her tracks. Something wasn't right. As she glanced around the room, her eyes fell on the door to the spare bedroom. She always kept it shut. For some reason, the latch wouldn't catch properly unless she jiggled the door handle the right way. And now, the door was open slightly, as if someone had tried to close it but without knowing the trick. Lillian always made sure it was closed properly. Which only meant one thing.

Someone had been in her apartment.

Lillian looked around again. Was the person still here? She backed toward the door and entered 911 into her phone. Leaving and calling the police was the obvious thing to do. Her finger hovered over the screen, but she didn't press call. Instead, Lillian stood in place and listened. Her apartment was completely silent. And it looked undisturbed at first glance. Was this just like her office at work? Had her home been searched, but nothing had been taken?

Keeping her phone in her hand and her thumb close to the call button, Lillian walked over to the spare room and opened the door. No one was in there. She entered each room in her apartment, one by one. Every one of them was empty. She let out a sigh of relief. Whoever had been in her house was no longer here.

Lillian went back to her bedroom and into her walk-in closet and removed a handful of dresses from one of the racks. Set into the wall behind it was a small safe. She didn't keep much in there—some jewelry, important documents, emergency cash. If this were some kind of professional robbery, it would have been the first thing the thieves would have gone for. And it had to be a professional. Her building had excellent security.

She examined the safe door. It showed no evidence of being tampered with. Lillian entered the combination and opened the safe. Everything was still in there. She went back into her bedroom and opened the jewelry box on her dresser. It was all there too. Whoever was in here wasn't looking for valuables.

She backtracked through the house, checking every room. Nothing had been taken. But there were minor signs of disturbance everywhere. The rarely used side table in the living room was clean of dust when there should have been a week or two of buildup. The fibers in the rug, indented by a foot far bigger than hers. Even the bottom drawer of her dresser, which mostly contained lingerie, appeared to have been looked through carefully, a thought which made her shudder.

Someone had searched through her things. And they did a thorough job of it too.

Lillian returned to the living room and sat down on her couch. The building was supposed to have twenty-four-hour security as well as a state-of-the-art digital security system. No one should have been able to get up to her floor, let alone her apartment, in the first place. There were security cameras in the lobby that could be checked. And she could ask the doorman if he'd let any strangers in. But that seemed improbable. All of this seemed improbable.

Was she imagining all this? Was she having some kind of nervous breakdown from all the stress? That would have been much simpler than the reality. Someone was watching her. And that someone was looking for something.

Who could it possibly be? There were so many options. A disgruntled colleague whose advances she'd rejected? A former client, or someone who had been on the receiving end of one of her client's lawsuits? She'd worked on plenty of high-stakes cases and pissed off a lot of powerful people. Her actions had indirectly caused people to lose their companies, or lose their fortunes, or end up in jail. They deserved it of course. But she wouldn't be surprised if they held a grudge.

It could even be from within her firm, which would make more sense considering that her office had been searched and her work laptop hacked. Thomas Jr. was the obvious choice. He openly despised her. Or, it could be someone else at work. An associate, jealous of Lillian's success. Someone she'd treated badly.

Whoever it was, what was it they wanted? To get revenge? To hurt Lillian somehow? And what were they looking for? Information? Dirt on her? They wouldn't find anything. Lillian always did everything by the book. She had nothing to hide.

Except for Emma.

Shit. Emma was her only secret. If someone found evidence of their relationship, they could use it to make Lillian lose her job. At least, if that was their goal.

But losing her job wasn't what worried Lillian. Whoever this was had stalked Lillian. They'd broken into her laptop. They'd invaded her home. They'd proven they weren't above breaking the law. And if they found out about Emma, they would know that she was Lillian's one weakness.

Just how far were they willing to go to get to Lillian?

26

LILLIAN

*L*illian picked up her phone and summoned Emma to her office. She walked over to the window and stared out at the city while she waited. She hadn't had a moment to herself all morning, but things had calmed down now. There was no point delaying the inevitable.

As soon as Emma entered the room, her face fell. "Something's wrong, isn't it?"

"Emma," Lillian said. "I didn't want to have this conversation at the office, but I didn't think it was safe to meet you outside of work."

"What are you talking about? You're scaring me, Lillian."

"Someone broke into my apartment over the weekend," Lillian said.

"What?" Emma took Lillian's hand. "Are you okay?"

"Yes. Nothing was taken. But I could tell that someone had been in there. I think they were looking for something." Lillian slipped her hand out of Emma's and took a few steps back.

Emma didn't notice. "Did you call the police?"

183

"And tell them what? That someone broke into my house and went through my drawers but didn't take anything? And they left no sign that they'd even been there? The police couldn't do anything with that information."

"I suppose you're right. But why would someone break into your house? What could they be looking for?"

"I don't know," Lillian said. "It's complicated."

"Then explain it to me."

Lillian rubbed her temples. "Someone has been following me. Or, they have someone following me for them. It's been going on for a while now. It's the same someone who went through my office. And they hacked my laptop. I know it sounds crazy. At first, I thought I was being paranoid, but it's impossible to ignore the facts. Someone is out to get me."

"Who could be after you?" Emma asked.

"I don't know. A stalker of some kind, maybe. A disgruntled ex-client, or someone a client of mine sued. I've been in this business long enough to have made my fair share of enemies. It could be someone here at the office."

"Lillian, you have to go to the police."

"I'm handling it," Lillian said. "But that isn't what I wanted to talk about. Whoever this person is, they're determined enough to have me followed around the city and to break into my house. They're more than willing to play dirty. I wouldn't put it past them to try to get to me in other ways. Like though you."

"What are you saying?" Emma's voice quavered.

"I'm saying that I don't want you to get caught up in this. That's why you need to resign from AG&W now. And we need to stop seeing each other. It's only temporary."

"What?" Emma paled. "No. Absolutely not."

"I'm sorry, Emma," Lillian said. "But I'm not taking any chances. I need you out of harm's way. Just until all this blows over."

"And how long is that going to take? When is this going to end? You won't even go to the police."

"I said, I'm handling it."

"And what, I'm just supposed to wait around, unable to contact you? Wondering if you're okay, wondering how long it will be until I can see you again?" Emma asked.

"Dammit Emma, do you think this is what I want? I'm trying to protect you."

"From what? You don't even know what's going on. And what about you, Lillian? You're the one who this person is targeting. You need me right now more than ever. We can work this out together."

Lillian let out an exasperated sigh. "You're so naive! This is serious, Emma. You can't just take my hand and say everything is going to be okay this time. Sometimes it's like you don't even live in the real world."

"You think that I'm naive?" Emma asked, her voice rising. "You think that I don't know anything about the real world?"

"Emma, I—"

"Have you forgotten everything that I told you about the past ten years of my life? About everything that I've sacrificed, everything that I've been through, everything that I've had to do?" Emma's eyes filled with angry tears. "Sure, maybe sometimes I seem naive and idealistic. But just because I don't go through life letting everything weigh me down doesn't mean I don't know what it's like to face problems that make everything seem hopeless. So don't tell me that I don't know how the real world works."

"You're right," Lillian said. "I'm sorry, I shouldn't have said that. It was unfair."

Emma took Lillian's hand again. "I know that you're scared," she said. "But pushing me away isn't going to help."

Lillian should have known Emma wasn't going to just roll over and accept this. "Fine. But this doesn't change the fact that there's something going on. I need time to think, to figure out what my next move is. Can you give me that?"

"Okay," Emma said. "But I'm not leaving AG&W. I'm not leaving you in the middle of this."

"All right. But we need to be even more careful."

Emma nodded. "I can do that."

Lillian sat down at her desk. "I need a moment to myself."

"Okay. I'll be here if you need me." Emma gave Lillian's hand one final squeeze and left the room.

Lillian leaned back in her chair and closed her eyes. She didn't feel good about this, but Emma wasn't giving her much of a choice. Or perhaps Lillian was just selfish and wanted to keep Emma close, despite everything.

She needed a plan. But she didn't have time to make one right now. Her paperwork was piling up, and she had deadlines looming. Regardless of what else was going on, she had a job to do.

The day wore on, and by late afternoon, Lillian's mind was much clearer. Getting some work done definitely helped. Working on problems she could actually solve made her feel more focused, more in control.

Around 5 p.m., there was a knock on the door. It was Stuart from IT.

"Yes, Stuart?" Lillian desperately hoped he had good news.

"I've been examining your laptop some more," he said. "I found something. Well, a couple of things. For starters, I was able to determine that the virus was installed locally, not remotely. Probably using a USB flash drive."

"You mean, whoever did this must have accessed my laptop in person," she said. It had to be here in the office. It was the only place she ever left her laptop unattended.

"Yes. But that's not all. As I expected from this kind of virus, its purpose was to log your activities and look through your files. But I found something else." Stuart paused, a solemn expression on his face. "The virus installed a script. It's like a program that delivers a set of instructions to the computer. The script was designed so that it could be triggered remotely. It never was activated. But the point of the script was that when triggered, it would download several gigabytes of illegal files from the internet."

"Why would it do something like that?" Lillian asked.

"Possessing these kinds of files is a felony," Stuart said. "An anonymous tip to the police and…"

And Lillian would be looking at criminal charges. She cursed. "You said the program was never triggered, right?"

"No, it wasn't."

"Have you told anyone else about this?" Lillian asked.

"No," Stuart replied. "I was the only one working on it. I'm supposed to write up a report and inform the security team, but I thought I'd tell you first."

"Can you keep it to yourself for now?"

"I don't know..." Stuart shifted awkwardly on the spot.

"You said yourself that it wasn't a company-wide security risk," Lillian said. "I'm the only one who's affected by this."

"But if there's someone in the office doing this kind of thing, shouldn't we do something about it?" Stuart asked.

"I will do something about it," Lillian said. "But I need some time. Give me the weekend, at least." It was Thursday. That would give her a few days to figure this out.

Stuart sighed. "Okay."

"Thank you, Stuart. Really, I mean it."

As Stuart left Lillian's office, she began to feel the gravity of what he'd told her. There was someone out there, probably in this very office, who was willing to frame her in order to have her wrongfully imprisoned. This was much worse than she thought.

27

EMMA

*E*mma made her way to work the next day, her stomach churning. Lillian was dealing with all this, but there was nothing Emma could do to help her. She couldn't even try to comfort Lillian in any way. She felt so powerless.

Emma stopped at the coffee shop like she did every morning. She didn't even notice when Bridget sidled up beside her until Bridget had said her name three times.

"Is everything okay?" Bridget asked.

"Yeah, it's fine," Emma replied. "I've just got a lot on my mind right now."

"Anything you want to talk about?"

Emma wished she could tell Bridget what was going on. Instead, Emma gave her a small, reassuring smile. "I'm okay. But thanks."

They picked up their coffee and walked the few blocks to the office. Bridget spent the entire time talking, so Emma didn't have to make conversation. She couldn't stop thinking about how withdrawn Lillian had seemed when she'd left work the previous day. She hoped Lillian was okay.

They arrived at the office, where Bridget took a seat behind the reception desk.

"Are you sure you're all right?" she asked.

Emma nodded. "I'm okay."

"Well, I'm always around if you need to talk."

"Thanks, Bridget."

Emma made her way to Lillian's office. When she entered the room, she was met with a stone-faced Lillian sitting behind her desk. Emma's stomach dropped.

Lillian didn't give her a chance to speak. "I need you to resign from AG&W today."

"What? Why? Has something happened?" Emma asked. "Talk to me, Lillian."

"It doesn't matter what happened. What matters is that whoever is out to get me is serious about taking me down. They're dangerous. You need to leave, and we need to cut contact entirely."

"You're in danger, and you're asking me to abandon you?" Emma asked. "I can't do that. We can work something out—"

"Just stop, Emma!" Lillian stood up and began pacing behind her desk. "We're not having this conversation again. My mind is already made up."

"Don't I get a say in this?"

"No. Too much is at stake. I need you as far away from me as possible."

"This is crazy," Emma said. "I'm not leaving you, Lillian."

"I'm not giving you a choice," Lillian replied. "You're fired."

Lillian's words were like a slap in the face. "What?"

"You heard me." Lillian's voice was devoid of emotion. "Now go."

"How can you just…" Emma trailed off. What had happened? Why did Lillian want Emma gone this badly? A thought emerged from the depths of her mind. "Is this really about keeping me safe? Or is it about your job? Is that why you don't want whoever is digging through your life to find out about us?"

Moments passed in silence. Lillian turned her head toward the window, her face half hidden from view. Emma's heart sank. Why wasn't Lillian saying anything? Why wasn't she denying it?

"I warned you about this," Lillian said. "I told you that my career will always come first. That's never going to change. Not for anything. Not for anyone. I'm not going to risk my job over a silly affair."

"You don't mean that. Lillian, please." Emma searched Lillian's eyes for just a hint of something, anything that showed that Lillian still cared for her. That the Lillian she knew was still in there somewhere. But her eyes were cold and empty.

Tears spilled onto Emma's cheeks. "You know, when I started working here, everyone warned me about you. They called you cold and heartless, and said that you don't care about anyone. I didn't believe them. Because you weren't like that with me. You were different with me. I thought maybe you…"

"I told you who I was from the start, Emma," Lillian said quietly.

Lillian's words sucked all the air out of the room. Emma

had to get out of there. Blinking away her tears, she stumbled to the door.

As she reached for the door handle, Emma paused, her back to Lillian. "Just so you know, the reason you're so cynical, and bitter, and miserable? It's your own fault! You've chosen this path in life that you hate, but you're too afraid to do anything about it. You're digging your own grave and you're too stubborn to stop."

With those parting words, Emma fled from Lillian's office. She grabbed her things, desperately trying to hold back her tears. She heard Bridget calling to her as she dashed to the elevator. Bridget would want to know what was wrong. What would Emma tell her? That Ms. White had fired her, just like all her other assistants? Clearly, that was all she was to Emma. Another assistant. Emma had been so stupid to think that they could have a future together. Stupid to think Lillian could be her happy ending.

Emma managed to keep herself together for long enough to hail a cab. As soon as she got in, she burst into tears. The cab driver, a tiny old man, reached back and handed her a box of tissues. He didn't say anything, but he gave her a slight smile. They drove along, the silence punctuated only by Emma's sobs.

By the time Emma reached her apartment, her tears had stopped, and she was left with a hollow feeling in the base of her chest. The old cab driver gave her one last, sympathetic smile before driving off. She must have looked like a mess.

She made her way up to her apartment. All she wanted to do was curl up in bed and forget about everything. Forget about Lillian, forget about AG&W, forget about this stupid city. She should have never moved here in the first place. If she hadn't, none of this would have happened.

Emma unlocked her door and entered her apartment. As she placed her things on the table, she heard a loud creak coming from her bedroom. She froze. Her building was old and sometimes made strange noises. That had to be all that it was, right?

She glanced toward her bedroom and couldn't see anything unusual. But her hairs were standing up on her skin, and her heart was pounding. Slowly, she tiptoed to her room.

Emma froze in the doorway. A few feet away, a large man dressed in a dark jacket and jeans was bent over Emma's dresser. His navy-blue baseball cap shrouded his face in shadow, and he was rooting through her top drawer, his hands covered in black gloves. He turned his head toward her.

Run, Emma's instincts told her. But her body wouldn't obey. As the man's eyes met hers, time seemed to slow down. At first, he seemed as surprised to see Emma as she was to see him. Then he straightened up and charged for her. Emma tried to move, but she was still frozen in place. All she could do was stand there as this hulk of a man came barreling toward her. He reached out, grabbed her shoulders, and shoved her, hard.

She fell backward uncontrollably, the back of her head striking the edge of the table in the hall behind her. Pain flared inside Emma's skull and she fell into darkness.

28

LILLIAN

$\mathcal{L}$illian sat in the meeting room with Thomas and one of their clients, an oil magnate who was friends with Gordon Sr. Lillian and Thomas were working the case together. Of course, she had done most of the work, but since Thomas and the client were both part of the same exclusive country club, they were behaving as if Lillian wasn't even in the room.

It didn't bother her. She simply didn't care anymore. She hated her job. She hated this place and everything that it stood for. She hated that she'd wasted her whole life getting here. What Emma had said to her was right. Lillian was making herself miserable.

Lillian held back a sigh. The only good thing in her life had been Emma. And now she was gone, forever. After what Lillian had done, she doubted that Emma would ever forgive her. But she had no choice. Things had escalated. She had to keep Emma safe.

The best way to do that was to get to the bottom of this once and for all. Lillian had been doing some thinking about who was behind everything and was close to figuring it out. But she needed to be sure.

Thomas and the client burst out laughing. Had one of them made yet another crude joke? Lillian hadn't heard a word that either of them had said in the last ten minutes. Her phone buzzed in her pocket. She pulled it out and glanced down at it under the table.

Emma? Why would Emma be calling Lillian now? A wave of dread came over her. Something was wrong.

Lillian stood up. "Excuse me for a moment." Without waiting for a response, she left the meeting room and walked into the hall.

She answered the phone. "Emma?"

"Lillian?" Emma sounded faint.

"What's the matter?" The other end of the line was silent for what seemed like an eternity. Lillian's heart sped up. "Emma!"

"There was a man in my apartment."

Lillian's blood ran cold. "Is he still there?" It had been an hour or two since Emma had left the office.

"No. I'm pretty sure he's gone." Emma's words were slow and slurred. "It's just... it's hard to remember."

Lillian frowned. "Are you all right? Are you hurt?"

"I don't know. My head hurts."

"Did he hit you? Are you bleeding?"

"I don't think so. I can't remember what happened."

"Emma. I'm coming over there right now, but I need you to hang up and call 911. Tell them someone broke into your house and that you need medical attention. And the police. Can you do that?"

"Okay."

Lillian frowned. Emma didn't sound like she was taking anything Lillian said in. "Just try. Please. I'll be right there, I promise."

"Okay," Emma said.

Lillian hung up and rushed out to reception. "Bridget. Find me Emma's address."

"Is everything okay, Ms. White?" Bridget asked.

"Just do it. *Now.*"

As soon as Bridget wrote Emma's details down, Lillian snatched up the piece of paper, rushed toward the elevator, and dialed 911.

Lillian reached Emma's address and got out of the cab. A police car and an ambulance were already parked on the street out front. She made her way into the building and rushed up the stairs to Emma's apartment.

She burst through Emma's open front door, her heart in her throat. "Emma?"

Emma was sitting on the couch in her living room. A paramedic sat on the coffee table in front of her, shining a light into her eyes. Two policemen stood in the kitchen talking.

Lillian threw her arms around Emma. "Thank god you're all right."

"Lillian?" Emma said, her tone uncertain. "What are you doing here?"

"I told you I was coming when you called me."

"I don't remember calling you."

Lillian looked from Emma to the paramedic. "Is she okay?"

"Don't worry," he said. "It's probably just a concussion. Some confusion and memory loss from around the time of injury is normal." He clicked off his penlight. "Were you the one who called 911?"

"Yes, I'm her girlfriend." Lillian said it without thinking. She didn't miss the scowl that broke out on Emma's face when she did. "Is she going to be all right? Does she need to go to the hospital?"

"She should be fine. But since she can't tell us what happened, she should get checked out by a doctor just in case. The doctor will probably want to do a CT scan and some other tests to be safe."

Lillian was flooded with relief. "I'll take her." She wasn't letting Emma out of her sight.

The paramedic nodded. As he packed up his bag to leave, the police came over to talk to Lillian and Emma. They reassured Lillian that the house was empty, nothing was amiss, and they had tried to take a statement from Emma, but it was full of holes. She had no memory between arriving home to find a man in her house and the paramedics arriving.

The police took a statement from Lillian about what Emma had said to her on the phone, which wasn't any more helpful than Emma's account. Lillian considered telling them about everything that had been happening to her but decided against it. She had no doubt that it was connected to the man who had been in Emma's apartment, but she didn't want to bring the police in just yet. Besides, all she cared about right now was making sure that Emma was okay.

The police gave Emma a card, instructing her to call them if she remembered anything, then left, leaving Emma and Lillian alone in the apartment.

Lillian sat down on the couch next to Emma. "How are you feeling?"

Emma ignored Lillian's question. "What are you doing here?" Her voice had a sharp edge.

"You called me," Lillian said. "So, I came."

"I don't remember calling you. It must have been because I was confused." Emma crossed her arms. "You should leave."

"Look, I'm sorry—"

"You're sorry? Sorry isn't good enough. You threw me away to protect yourself, your job, and now what, you feel guilty?"

"I lied, Emma!" Lillian said. "It was all an act. I swear I was just trying to protect you."

"Why didn't you tell me that?" Emma's voice quavered. "Why did you make me believe that you cared about your job more than me?"

"It was the only way I could think of to get you to stay away," Lillian said. "I couldn't risk you getting involved. And I knew you wouldn't take no for an answer."

"Why should I believe you?"

"You're right. You have no reason to believe me. But it's the truth. My job, all of that, none of it matters. All I wanted was for you to be safe."

Emma grunted. "It didn't even work."

"I know," Lillian said. "And I'll never forgive myself for

letting you get hurt. I don't expect you to forgive me either. But you heard what the paramedic said. You need to get checked out. I'm taking you to the hospital."

"I'm fine. I'll go myself."

"No, you're not. I'm not letting you go alone."

"Then I'll find someone else to take me," Emma said.

"Emma." Lillian placed her hand on Emma's arm. "Please. Let me do this. It's the least I can do."

"Fine. But I'm still mad at you."

"You have every right to be. But you're going to have to put up with me for a little longer. After we're finished at the hospital, I'm taking you somewhere safe until this is all over."

There was a flicker of fear in Emma's eyes. "Do you think whoever is doing this is going to come back? Or do something else?"

"I don't think so, but I'm not taking any chances," Lillian replied. "And I won't let any harm come to you."

*E*mma woke up early on Saturday morning after a strange dream in which she was drowning in an enormous, plush bed. It wasn't far from reality. She pushed aside the covers and rolled onto her back. Her head ached. For a moment, Emma didn't know where she was. Then the events of the day before came rushing back to her.

After the police had left, Lillian took Emma to a modern-looking hospital where they were seen immediately. Emma made a comment about how much it would cost, but Lillian told her not to worry about anything. The doctor confirmed that she had nothing more than a concussion. She'd have a bad headache and some dizziness and irritability, but that was all.

Emma groggily rolled over. Lillian was fast asleep next to her, her long golden hair fanned out on the pillow behind her head. The doctor had instructed Lillian not to leave Emma alone for forty-eight hours, and to make sure that she rested. Emma was still furious with Lillian. She barely spoke a word to her at the hospital, and on the way back. But at the same time, she was grateful for Lillian's presence and her insistence that they go somewhere safe. Emma was shaken by everything that had happened, even though she didn't remember much. She didn't want to be alone, especially not in her house.

The safe place that Lillian had chosen for them was a hotel known for its high security due to its wealthy clientele. Lillian said she was just being cautious, but Emma appreciated it all the same. The fact that their suite was just as luxurious as the one they had stayed at in San Francisco was a bonus. By the time they arrived, it was evening. Emma had been so tired that she'd practically passed out on the huge bed immediately.

As Emma watched Lillian sleep, her chest rising and falling rhythmically, she found herself drifting off again. When Emma next awoke, it was midday, and she was alone in the room. She got up from the bed and was immediately hit by a wave of dizziness, so she sat back down. On her second try, she managed to stay on her feet. She made her way out of the bedroom.

"Lillian?" Emma looked around the living room.

"Emma." Lillian rushed out of the kitchen. "Are you all right? Do you need something?"

"I'm okay," Emma said.

"Then why are you out of bed?"

"I've been asleep for fifteen hours! I'm sick of being in bed."

"Emma, you're supposed to be resting." Lillian pointed at the bed.

Emma crossed her arms. "We're not at work. You don't get to boss me around."

Lillian raised an eyebrow. "This must be what the doctor meant when he said you might be irritable."

"This isn't funny, Lillian!"

"All right, I'm sorry." Lillian placed a hand on Emma's shoulder. "Will you get back into bed if I come sit with you?"

"Okay," Emma grumbled.

Lillian led her back to bed. After making sure that Emma was comfortable, Lillian got in next to her. After a moment, Emma rested her head on Lillian's shoulder.

"Does this mean you're not angry at me anymore?" Lillian asked.

"I don't know," Emma replied.

"You were right, you know. About everything. Pushing you away was a mistake. I was scared, and I wasn't thinking. And I shouldn't have treated you so cruelly. I'm sorry."

Emma sighed. It was clear that Lillian was tying herself in knots over this. "I can't stay mad at you forever. Honestly, I was so happy to see you when you walked through my door yesterday. Even with everything that happened, even though I was upset with you, when I was scared and alone, all I could think about was how much I wished you were there."

"I'm here now. And I'm not going anywhere." Lillian reached for Emma's hand and laced her fingers between Emma's.

"So what happens now?" Emma asked. "With us? With everything?"

"We can talk about it later," Lillian said. "You need to rest."

"For god's sake, Lillian. I have a concussion, I'm not dying."

"All right then. What do you want to happen next?"

"I don't know," Emma said. "But I don't want to go back to hiding our relationship."

"I don't want that either. From now on, no more hiding."

"Really? What about your job?"

"I don't give a damn about my job," Lillian said. "That's another thing you were right about. I've been making myself miserable for a long time."

Emma winced. "Sorry, I didn't mean to be so harsh."

"Everything you said was true. I've been too scared to step off the path I put myself on, even though it's killing me. I needed to hear it to accept it."

"Does this mean you're going to quit your job?"

"Not yet," Lillian said. "I'll figure that out once I've dealt with everything else."

"Everything else? You know who's behind all this?" Emma asked.

"I have a few ideas."

"Are you going to go to the police?"

"I will eventually," Lillian said. "But I don't have anything definitive to give them yet. They won't be able to do much. And I don't want to lose this opportunity."

"The opportunity for what?" Emma asked.

"To bring whoever is doing this down."

"Lillian? You're not going to do something dangerous are you?"

"I'm not, I promise," Lillian said. "But don't think for a

second that I'm going to let the person who did this get away with it. I don't care what dirty tricks they use to get to me. No one hurts the woman I love."

It took Emma a moment for Lillian's words to register in her mind. "You said *love*."

"Yes, I did. I love you, Emma."

"I…" Emma's heart skittered in her chest. "I love you, too."

Lillian took Emma's chin and planted a soft kiss on her lips. Emma's head started to spin all over again.

"My head still feels a little off," Emma said. "You might have to remind me that you love me again later, in case I forget. You know, with the memory loss and all."

Lillian smiled. "I love you. And I'm never going to let you forget." She kissed Emma again. "Now, it's really time for you to rest. Why don't we watch something? Last time we were in bed together, you said that you wanted to snuggle up and watch movies." Lillian reached over and picked up the remote control from beside the bed. "We can watch some of those romance movies I told you about."

"That sounds perfect," Emma said.

Lillian picked out a movie, one that she assured Emma she would enjoy. As soon as the movie began, Emma became so absorbed in it that she forgot all about her aching head, and all the crazy things that had happened. Soon, her anger toward Lillian disappeared completely.

Hours passed, and they watched another movie, then another. At some point, they ordered room service and had a decadent feast right there on the bed. It was heaven.

Between cuddling in bed with Lillian and watching women fall in love on screen over and over, Emma started to feel like her younger self again. The Emma who believed in love, and romance, and happily-ever-afters. Perhaps it was naive. But she was beginning to wonder if she'd been wrong when she'd given up on ever having her own fairy-tale ending.

30

EMMA

By Sunday, Emma was back to normal. Lillian insisted that she continue to rest, but she convinced Lillian to let her get out of bed. They continued their movie marathon, this time on the couch in the hotel suite.

Late in the afternoon, Lillian got up and announced she was going to take a shower.

As Lillian walked away, Emma grabbed her hand. "Why don't I join you?" she asked, peering up at Lillian.

"I don't think so," Lillian said. "The doctor said not to do anything strenuous. And I don't think we can get in the shower together without doing anything strenuous."

"It's been exactly forty-eight hours."

Lillian raised an eyebrow. "Have you been counting down the hours just for this?"

Emma shrugged. "Maybe."

A smile tugged at Lillian's lips. "Then let's go take a shower."

Emma got up and made her way to the bathroom,

pulling her loose cotton dress off on the way there. Lillian followed, shedding her own clothes.

By the time Lillian reached the bathroom, Emma was naked. Lillian removed her own bra and panties, dropping them to the floor with Emma's.

Emma drew Lillian into the shower. The large, futuristic-looking shower had a control panel on the wall, and there was no shower head above them. Lillian pressed a few buttons on the panel, and water fell from the ceiling like rain.

Emma closed her eyes and tilted her head back, letting the warm water flow over her face and down her hair. Wiping the water from her eyes, she caught a glimpse of Lillian through the rising steam. Droplets trickled down Lillian's body, her wet skin shimmering under the warm light.

Lillian cupped Emma's face in her hands and kissed her softly, as if Emma would break at the slightest touch. But when Emma drew back and looked into Lillian's eyes, she saw a hunger barely restrained.

"Lillian. I'm not made of glass." She wrapped her arms around Lillian's neck and spoke into her ear. "I need you to fuck me right now."

Emma's own words flooded her cheeks with heat, but they had the desired effect. Lillian pressed her lips against Emma's with a ferocity that made her heart race. She pinned Emma against the cold glass with her body, trapping Emma against it. Emma closed her eyes, surrendering to Lillian's overpowering embrace. Her hands slid over Lillian's wet skin as she tried impossibly to pull Lillian closer.

Lillian slid her leg between Emma's thighs, rolling her hips slowly, rhythmically. Emma rocked back against Lillian, eager to sate the hunger deep inside.

"Lillian," Emma murmured, delirious with desire.

Without warning, Lillian spun Emma around and pushed her up against the glass again. She pulled aside the damp hair that was plastered to the back of Emma's neck, and kissed, nibbled, and sucked her skin. Lillian's hand crept forward and down to stroke Emma's slit. If she wasn't already in the shower, she'd be dripping wet.

Lillian's lips brushed against Emma's ear. "Spread out your legs and put your hands on the glass."

Emma obeyed immediately. She turned her head to watch as Lillian unhooked a small shower head from the wall and turned it on. Warm water came blasting out of it. Lillian pulled Emma's hips away from the glass as Emma scooted her hips even further back, pressing her ass into Lillian.

Lillian guided the shower head around Emma's body, directing it down her stomach, lower and lower, until it finally reached her target. Lillian used her other hand to spread Emma's lips. Emma's whole body shuddered as the jet of water hit her sensitive bud.

Lillian ran her hand up the front of Emma's chest, grasping at her breasts and pinching her nipples gently between the sides of her fingers. Emma gasped with delight, grinding back against Lillian. Lillian kept her body tense, holding Emma in place.

As Emma writhed against her, Lillian slid her free hand down Emma's back, skimming her fingers all the way down to her entrance.

"Oh god, Lillian," Emma begged.

Emma let out a sound between a moan and a whimper as Lillian eased into her. Lillian's fingers slipped in easily, filling her completely. Emma braced herself against the slippery glass wall, her whole-body jolting as Lillian pierced her.

With the jet of water still directed at the crease of her thighs, it only took a few thrusts until Emma's pleasure peaked, sending wave after wave of orgasmic ecstasy through her.

"Mmm..." Emma's breathing slowed, and her body calmed. Her skin felt flushed from the steam.

Lillian dropped the shower head, spun Emma back around, and drew her in for a kiss. As the kiss deepened, a soft growl emerged from Lillian's chest.

Emma didn't need Lillian to speak to know what it meant. She ran her hands down the front of Lillian's chest, grazing Lillian's stiff, pink nipples with her fingertips. Emma continued down Lillian's stomach, her hips, and down to where her thighs met. She parted Lillian's lips with a fingertip and ran it up and down her velvety folds.

Emma glanced at Lillian through the sheets of falling water. "I want to taste you."

With a shuddering breath, Lillian closed her eyes and leaned back against the wall. "*Yes.*"

Before Emma knew it, she was on her knees. Water cascaded down the creases of Lillian's hips and thighs as she spread her feet apart. Her pale pink lips glistened enticingly.

Emma leaned in and kissed the baby-soft skin of Lillian's inner thighs. Lillian's sweet scent flooded her head. She kissed her way upward and slid her tongue into Lillian's slit, causing her to hiss softly.

Emma licked and sucked every inch of Lillian's folds, savoring her taste. It was indescribably complex, somehow sweet, salty, and sour all at once. And it drove Emma wild.

Lillian dropped her hands to Emma's head, her fingers twining through Emma's damp hair, a silent command not to stop. Emma worked away, her knees aching from the hard tile floor, relishing the effect she was having on Lillian. Every sound Lillian made, every shudder that went through her body, sent heat shooting through her.

Lillian's moans grew louder, and her hands pressed harder into the back of Emma's head as she thrust desperately against Emma's mouth. Then her thighs clamped around Emma and her whole body quaked, a string of curses flying from her lips.

Emma left the bathroom wrapped in a towel. They had spent the last hour in there, making up for lost time once again, until Lillian kicked Emma out because she wanted to have an actual shower. Apparently, she found Emma's naked, soapy body too distracting. Or maybe it was because Emma refused to keep her hands to herself.

She sat down on the edge of the bed and began searching through her bag for something to wear. As she pulled out her oversized sweatshirt, she noticed her phone half-buried under all the clothes. She had thrown it in her bag on Friday night, and with everything going on, she hadn't looked at it since.

Emma pressed the power button, but the battery was dead. She rooted around in her bag again until she found her charger, plugged it into the wall, then connected her phone. She grabbed a pair of jeans and threw them on with a T-shirt and the sweatshirt. By the time she was done getting dressed, her phone had enough power to turn itself on.

Emma unlocked the phone. She had a dozen missed calls from her mom, as well as a series of increasingly frantic texts. *Crap.* It was her sister's birthday today. Emma had completely forgotten about it. She had told her mom that she would drop by in the morning. It was evening now.

Emma dialed her mom's number. "Mom? Sorry I missed—"

"Emma? Are you all right?" her mom asked. "Where are you?"

"Mom, I'm fine." Emma told her mom a very censored version of what had happened on Friday.

"Oh my God, Emma. And you're up there all alone? I'm coming right now. I'll have to find someone to keep an eye on the kids—"

"It's okay, Mom. I'm okay. I'm not alone. I have Lillian. My girlfriend."

"Right. I forgot about her. Is she taking care of you?" her mom asked.

"She is. I'm in good hands, I promise," Emma replied.

"Okay. But I'm still coming up there to see you. I should be able to get some time off on Monday."

Emma's mom proceeded to fuss and worry over the phone. Emma could barely get a word in. After a while, the twins started yelling in the background, and her mom had to go.

"I'll talk to you later, Mom," Emma said.

"Rest up, okay honey?"

"Okay."

As soon as Emma hung up the phone, Lillian walked out of the bathroom wearing a bathrobe, her hair wrapped up in a towel.

"Lillian?"

Lillian sat down on the bed next to her. "Yes?"

"I just talked to my mom. I told her what happened, and she's insisting on coming to see me." Emma gave Lillian her sweetest look. "How do you feel about meeting my mom?"

Lillian didn't miss a beat. "I'd love to."

"Great. She already knows about the two of us. But I haven't mentioned that you're my boss... well, soon-to-be-former boss. She might need some time to adjust." Emma's mom was also under the impression that her boss was a bit of a tyrant. Emma would have to talk to her mom beforehand. "She's coming tomorrow."

"That's fine," Lillian said. "But I have to take care of things in the morning first."

The look on Lillian's face was clear: She was on the warpath. And Emma didn't envy whoever got in her way.

31

LILLIAN

*L*illian marched into the AG&W offices. It was time to get to end this once and for all. Ignoring Bridget's customary greeting, she made her way to Thomas's office. She reached for the door handle, ready to charge in, then knocked instead. She had to be tactful if she wanted him to cooperate.

"Come in," Thomas said.

She opened the door and walked inside.

"Lillian? You missed the partners' meeting this morning."

"I know." She sat down in front of his desk. "I was with Emma."

"What?" Thomas blinked rapidly. "Are you admitting that the two of you are together?"

"Someone broke into her apartment on Friday and knocked her unconscious."

"Shit, is she okay?"

Lillian's stomach sank. His surprise seemed genuine. It would have been much easier if Thomas were behind everything. "She's fine. But I have reason to believe that someone in this office was responsible for it. Among other things, like breaking into my apartment."

Thomas crossed his arms. "Let me guess? You think it was me?"

"No. I don't think you did this."

"You don't?"

"You're not stupid enough to break the law over a petty workplace feud." Lillian had concluded that the culprit was someone who had something to gain from her losing her job. But she suspected that they were acting out of desperation rather than maliciousness. If whoever was doing this wanted her to suffer, they could have triggered the virus on her laptop and had her arrested.

"Then why are you telling me this?" Thomas asked.

"Because I need you to know how serious this is," Lillian said. "Because I'm going to ask you a question, and you're going to answer it honestly."

"Sure, anything."

Lillian was surprised by how cooperative Thomas was being. Maybe he wasn't as much of an asshole as she thought. "Who did you tell about Emma and me?"

"No one," Thomas said.

"Are you sure? Not Bridget? Not your drinking buddies?"

"Yes, I'm sure. Wait." Thomas furrowed his brows. "Avery. We had a few drinks together a couple of weeks ago. I wasn't planning on telling him; it just slipped out."

Lillian's blood ran cold.

"Hold on. You don't think he did this, do you?"

"Where is Avery now?" Lillian asked.

"He's in a meeting with the guys from Hammond Industries," Thomas replied. "Lillian? This is crazy. Why would Avery do something like that?"

Lillian got up from her chair. "Thank you, Thomas."

Ignoring Thomas's protests, Lillian left his office and made her way to the meeting room. *Avery*. He'd always been unscrupulous, despite the image he projected to the world. But Lillian never thought he'd turn on her.

Lillian stormed into the meeting room. "Avery. I need to speak with you. *Now*."

Avery turned to her. "Lillian? Can't you see that I'm in the middle of a meeting?"

"I don't give a damn."

The men sitting around the table shifted in their seats.

Avery placated them with a half-smile. "Excuse me for a moment, gentlemen." He joined Lillian in the hallway, shutting the door carefully behind him. "Have you gone insane?"

"I was about to ask you the same thing," Lillian said.

"What the fuck is going on?"

"We should talk in my office."

"Lillian. I have *the* Hammond from Hammond Industries in there. Whatever it is, it can wait."

"No, it can't," Lillian said. "You're going to come with me right now. Or I'm going to go into that meeting room and announce to Hammond that AG&W is so far in the red that his money is the only thing keeping us from going bankrupt."

Avery blanched. "You're serious?"

"Do I look like I'm joking?"

Avery pinched the bridge of his nose. "Give me a moment." He opened the meeting room door and stuck his head inside. "There's a small emergency that I need to go deal with. I'll be right back."

Hammond did not look impressed. Nevertheless, Avery followed Lillian to her office. She shut the door behind him and sat behind her desk.

"You have one minute to tell me what the hell this is about," Avery said.

"You're not in a position to make demands, Avery," Lillian said.

"What's that supposed to mean?"

"I know that you're behind the break-in at my apartment, as well as Emma's. I know that you're having me followed. And I know that you hacked my laptop."

"What are you talking about?" Avery asked.

"Don't play dumb with me. You know damn well what I'm talking about."

"No, I don't."

For a moment, Lillian wondered whether she'd gotten it all wrong. Avery's surprise seemed just as genuine as Thomas's. But then she remembered how good Avery was at bending the truth. After all, he'd taught Lillian everything he knew.

"Avery. If you don't start talking, not only will I tell Hammond about our finances, I'll tell every single one of our other clients."

"You're talking about sinking this firm because, what, you think I broke into your apartment? Do you have any idea how crazy you sound right now, Lillian?" Avery's expression transformed into one of concern. "You've been under a lot of pressure lately. It sounds like the stress might be getting to you. Maybe you should see someone."

"Cut the shit, Avery. The woman I love was hurt because of you. I'm not playing games. I will sink this firm if I have to." Lillian had only meant the words as a threat. But as she said them, she realized they were true.

Avery stared at her, his face slowly darkening. "You're bluffing. That would be career suicide."

"Do I look like I'm bluffing?" Lillian held his gaze. "Start talking. Now."

"Fine. Fine!" Avery held up his hands in resignation. "I was trying to figure out a way to force you to resign. Are you happy?"

Lillian's heart sank. "Why, Avery? After all these years. Why?"

"Because the firm is in trouble. It's not going to survive much longer. I've looked into every option. And the only one left is a merger with Browne & Associates."

"Let me guess. The merger means that someone will have to step down as partner?"

"Yes," Avery replied. "There isn't enough room for all three of us at the top."

"But why me? Thomas is one of the worst attorneys to ever work at AG&W. And he's barely been a partner for a year."

"It isn't me who wants you to step down," Avery said. "It's Browne. You've met him, haven't you?"

"Yes." Lillian had disliked him from the start. But she would have sucked it up to work with him like she always did. At least, the old Lillian would have.

"You know how conservative he is. Thomas comes from an established family of attorneys going back generations.

219

The Gordon name holds weight. And Brown thought he'd be a better fit for the culture of the firm."

"The culture?" Lillian scoffed. "Do you mean the fact that the entire firm is made up of wealthy white men?"

"Those were his words, not mine," Avery said. "Given the choice between the two of you, he's insisting that Thomas take the remaining senior partner position. But I knew you'd never agree to step down."

"You're damn right I wouldn't."

"That's why I had to take matters into my own hands," Avery said. "I built this firm up from nothing. I've poured decades of my life into it. I just couldn't let it go under. It's nothing personal."

The room fell silent. There was a thin sheen of sweat on Avery's forehead.

"Start from the beginning," Lillian said. "Tell me everything you did. I want the truth. Unless you want me to start calling clients?"

"No." Avery sighed. "I hired a private investigator to look into you. I was trying to find dirt that I could use to invoke the 'inappropriate conduct' clause of your contract. Everyone has dirt, Lillian. Except for you, apparently. Then, when Thomas told me there was something going on between you and Emma, I knew it was true. He was spot on about your behavior toward her being unusual. So I had the PI look into Emma as well."

"You went digging through Emma's life too? You had her followed?"

"Yes. I thought that she was far more likely to slip up than you."

Lillian's blood boiled. Emma hadn't even noticed. Hell,

Lillian had only noticed she was being followed because everything else that was happening had made her paranoid. They were lucky that Thomas didn't tell Avery about the two of them before they went to San Francisco together. They had been so brazen about their relationship while they were there. She had no doubt he would have sent someone to watch them if he'd known.

"But neither of you gave anything away, and it became clear to the PI that you were starting to catch on. That's when I got desperate." Avery averted his eyes. "I had him to break into your apartment to see if he could find anything. He was mostly looking for evidence that you were having a relationship with Emma."

"Private investigators don't break into private properties," Lillian said. "They have to follow the law, just like everyone else."

"Some of them will do anything for a price. He didn't find anything in the end. You were too careful. So I had him look through Emma's apartment. She wasn't meant to be there, Lillian. Someone else was supposed to watch her and make sure she didn't leave work. My guy got spooked—"

"Your guy got spooked by a 110-pound woman, so he knocked her out and left her alone and unconscious on the fucking floor?" Lillian asked.

"That's not how it happened."

"Did he even check to see if she was still breathing? Or did he simply leave her there, not caring whether she was even alive or not?"

"It was an accident, Lillian, I swear," Avery said. "She was never meant to get hurt."

"What the hell did you think would happen when you hired a criminal to do your dirty work?"

"I know, okay!" Avery put his head in his hands. "I never meant for any of this to happen. But she's fine, isn't she?"

"You already know that Emma is fine," Lillian said. "I'm sure you have someone keeping an eye on things."

"Only because I had to know if she was okay. I feel terrible."

"What about the virus on my laptop? The program to download illegal files? Were you going to activate it, then call the police on me so that I get thrown into jail?"

"No, I was never planning to use it. It was a last resort. I never triggered it, and I never would have, I swear. I didn't want you in jail. I just wanted you gone from AG&W. That's all. I didn't want to do any real damage. I didn't want anyone to actually get hurt," he said again.

Lillian let the silence stretch out. Avery's guilt was genuine. He was too proud to fake any vulnerability. She didn't give a damn about his feelings. Not after what he did to Emma. But she could use this.

Lillian got up from her desk and began to pace behind it. "You've just confessed to a number of felonies," she said. "Conspiracy, accessory to burglary, assault, not to mention various cybercrimes."

Avery lifted his head from his hands and opened his mouth to protest.

Lillian held up a finger. "On the other hand, I've just admitted to a relationship with Emma. I won't deny it any longer. Which means that you and Thomas have every right to push me out. But you're not going to do that." Lillian placed her hands on the desk and leaned toward him.

"Here's what's going to happen. You're going to give me two weeks to get everything in order. When those two weeks are up, I'll resign. With a generous severance package, of course. And then you'll have your merger."

Avery frowned. "That's it? You're not going to go to the police?"

"Not if you keep to our agreement." Lillian hoped that Avery was too shaken to notice all the holes in her logic. "We both know the police won't find anything to connect you to this. I'm sure you've covered your tracks well, this time at least. But you said it yourself. Everyone has dirt. What will I find if I start digging through yours? Something the police will be interested in hearing about? The IRS? The FBI maybe?"

Avery paled. This time, Lillian was bluffing. But clearly, she'd hit a nerve.

"All right," he said. "We have a deal."

Lillian smiled. "You'd better get back to your meeting."

"Shit." Avery stood up and headed for the door. "Look, Lillian, I'm really sorry. About Emma especially."

"If you ever do anything to hurt Emma again," Lillian said, "if you ever go near her again, I will bring this entire fucking firm crashing down on your head."

"I won't. I promise."

Lillian watched Avery leave her office. She was going to bring him down anyway. All in due time.

32

EMMA

*E*mma walked into the new office of Lillian White
& Associates. Renovations had just finished, and
everything looked modern and new, but not in a sterile way
like AG&W had. It was much smaller, and nowhere near the
top floor of the building, but it was still impressive.

Bridget sat at the reception desk typing away, the phone
balanced on one shoulder. She smiled at Emma as she
passed. When Emma had told her that Lillian was her girlfriend and they'd been having a secret relationship, Bridget
had almost fainted. That juicy bit of gossip had almost
eclipsed all the other drama that had come with AG&W's
downfall.

It was just over a month since Lillian had confronted
Avery. Lillian had been true to her word. She'd continued
working at AG&W for two weeks after the incident and had
resigned right on schedule. What Avery didn't know at the
time was that Lillian had been working behind the scenes to
set up her new firm, and she'd convinced several her loyal
clients to come with her.

The loss of Lillian's clients hit AG&W hard. When it became clear just how much trouble AG&W was in, Browne and Associates rescinded their offer of a merger, and the firm went under. It was a ruthless move on Lillian's part. But, in her words, AG&W was rotten to the core. Their demise was inevitable—Lillian had just helped it along.

Emma continued through to the offices. The desks were empty, save for Stuart, the new head of IT, who was setting up the computers. In a week's time when the firm opened, it would be filled with all of Lillian's employees, most of whom had worked at AG&W. After AG&W went under, Lillian had been more than happy to provide them with jobs. Lillian had poured everything she owned into this new firm. She needed all the help she could get if she wanted it to be successful

Emma herself had turned down the job that Lillian had found her in order to work at Lillian's firm. But what Emma hasn't told Lillian yet was that she had other plans. All the craziness of the past few months had forced Emma to take a good, hard look at her life. She didn't want to work in a law firm forever, especially not one as hectic as Lillian's. Emma wanted to find her passion, just like Lillian had. And she couldn't do that while working for her girlfriend.

She made her way to Lillian's office. The door was ajar, and the room was empty. Lillian had told Emma she would be in the office all day, so she couldn't have gone far. Emma sat down in front of Lillian's desk and placed the bag she was carrying on the table. Her eyes fell on Lillian's chair. She wondered what Lillian would do if she returned to her office and found Emma sitting behind her desk. She tried to push the thought aside. Emma was here to tell Lillian her news, not to play games with her.

But that didn't mean that she couldn't do both. A naughty plan began to form in Emma's mind.

A moment later, Lillian walked into the room, her phone held up to her ear in one hand, and a cup of coffee in the other. She wore a dark pantsuit, and her stylish blonde bob practically shone. Emma still wasn't used to Lillian's new hairstyle, but she liked it much better than that strict bun Lillian used to sport every day.

"If you insist on taking this case to trial, that's fine with me," Lillian said. "But there isn't a judge in this whole damn city who's going to believe your client's story. So I suggest that you convince him to agree to mediation, or we'll counter-sue for the emotional distress that this ridiculous lawsuit has caused my client!" Without waiting for a response, Lillian hung up the phone.

She sat down in her chair and placed the coffee cup on her desk. Without saying a word, she beckoned Emma to her side, then pulled Emma into her lap for a deep, steamy kiss.

Emma exhaled slowly. "Wow. What was that for?"

"Do I need a reason to kiss my girlfriend?" Lillian asked.

"You do if you're going to kiss me like that."

"I'm in a good mood," Lillian said. "Everything's coming together. The office is ready ahead of schedule. I finally convinced the representative of that class-action suit to continue working with me here. And to top it off, I've just heard that Avery was taken into custody."

"Really?" Emma asked. "Didn't you say that there wasn't enough evidence to make the charges stick?"

"There wasn't," Lillian said. "Not initially. But I've been in contact with a private investigator I used on some of my cases. I told him all about what happened. It turns out that PIs don't like when one of their own breaks the law for money. He tracked down the PI Avery hired. It turns out Avery wasn't the only client he was doing dirty work for. My PI placed an anonymous tip and had him arrested. He confessed to performing illegal work for Avery, as well as several others, in exchange for a shorter sentence. His confession is more than enough to get Avery charged."

"That's amazing," Emma said. "Aren't you afraid he'll retaliate?"

"No," Lillian replied. "Avery isn't that kind of man. He was just desperate. But when someone as powerful and arrogant as him gets desperate, people get hurt. I wasn't going to let him get away with what he did."

Emma remembered the bag on the desk. "I brought you lunch. I thought you could use a home-cooked meal." Emma and Lillian had been spending plenty of time together now that their relationship was out in the open. And Emma had quickly learned that Lillian didn't know how to cook, which explained her diet of takeout and coffee. It was amusing that someone as together as Lillian was so hopeless in certain areas of her life.

"It smells delicious," Lillian said. "You're spoiling me."

"I have an ulterior motive," Emma replied. "I wanted to have lunch with you."

"Sure. But first, what was it that you wanted to tell me?"

"Right. My mom called. She invited us to come down for Thanksgiving."

"That sounds… lovely," Lillian said.

"Don't worry, I made her promise she won't give you the third degree again."

It turned out that her mother's interest in Emma's romantic life hadn't ended with her last relationship. Once she'd come to terms with the fact that Emma and Lillian were a couple, Emma's mom had become so heavily invested that it was only a matter of time before she started asking when the two of them were getting married. Although Lillian didn't say anything, Emma suspected she was intimidated by it all.

"Tell her I said I'd love to," Lillian said.

"Okay," Emma said. "But that's not all I wanted to tell you. I know I said that I'd come work for you here, but I've changed my mind."

"Is that all? I was worried that it was something serious."

"You're not disappointed?" Emma asked.

"Of course not. I am going to miss having you around all day, but I'll live. So why can't you work for me? It sounds like you have something else in mind."

"I do," Emma said. "I've finally figured out what I want to do with my life. I want to be a social worker. I've spent so much of my life caring for others. Over the last few months, I've started to miss it."

"Is that why you're constantly trying to mother me?" Lillian teased.

"I'm serious, Lillian. Whether it's because of my family situation or not, I have this innate desire to help people, to support them. It's what I'm good at, so that's what I'm going to do."

"That sounds like the perfect career for you. You'll make a wonderful social worker."

"Thanks. I've been looking into the requirements, and with community college under my belt, it will only take me two years to get my degree." Emma said. "And you'll be happy to know I've already found a replacement legal assistant. Her name is Jean, and she has fifteen years' experience working as a legal secretary, and a long list of glowing references. She can start on Monday. And she always uses Oxford commas."

"She sounds perfect. You always know exactly what I need."

"That's why you love me."

"Among other reasons," Lillian said, kissing her again.

"You know…" Emma peered at Lillian from under her eyelashes and gave the other woman her sultriest smile. "I'm going to miss working for you. Sneaking away, getting all hot and heavy in that fancy bathroom of yours. Calling you Ms. White."

A blue-hot flame sparked behind Lillian's eyes. "You can still call me Ms. White. And there isn't anywhere to sneak away to here. But I have this perfectly good office."

Emma's pulse began to race, and her eyes fixed on Lillian's. She got up from Lillian's lap, pushed her laptop aside, and sat down on top of the desk. "What are you suggesting, Ms. White?"

Lillian got up from her chair and seized Emma by the waist, positioning herself between Emma's knees. She leaned in close, her lips tickling Emma's ear. "I'm suggesting that I'm going to fuck you on my desk."

Lillian's words flooded Emma's body with heat. She pressed her lips to Lillian's, devouring her. Lillian drew Emma in, kissing her back with the force of her entire body.

She stripped Emma's jacket from her shoulders and swept her hands up Emma's sides, all the way from her hips up to her breasts.

Emma broke the kiss. "What if someone comes in?"

"Do you want me to stop?" Lillian asked, her hands creeping up Emma's thigh underneath her dress.

"No, don't stop."

Lillian tugged at the straps of Emma's dress, drawing them down her shoulders along with her bra straps. She pushed the bra and dress down Emma's chest, exposing her breasts to the cool air. Lillian leaned down and covered one of Emma's pebbled nipples with her mouth, dragging her tongue over it, then sucking firmly. Emma let out a cry.

Lillian pressed a finger to Emma's lips. "Do you want the whole office to hear us?" she asked.

Emma shook her head.

"Then don't make a sound," Lillian whispered.

Emma nodded.

Lillian continued to lavish attention on Emma's breasts, her hands and mouth working in tandem. Emma swallowed her moans until they began to build up in her chest.

"Lillian," she said softly, "I need you."

Lillian straightened up and pushed Emma's shoulders down toward the desk. Emma propped herself up on her elbows and watched as Lillian ran her hands down to the hem of her dress. Her eyes never leaving Emma's, Lillian pushed Emma's dress up her thighs.

Emma lifted her hips, allowing Lillian to peel off her panties. Lillian dropped them on the floor at her feet, then yanked Emma's hips toward her, sliding her bare ass along the desk until she was right at the edge of it. Lillian bent over and kissed Emma, her thigh pressing hard between Emma's legs. She glided her hands down Emma's stomach slowly.

"Lillian," Emma said. "I need you."

Lillian pushed Emma's knees apart and traced her hands up Emma's inner thighs slowly.

"Lillian, please."

Lillian parted Emma's lips and stroked her silky folds.

Emma quivered. "Lillian…"

Slowly, Lillian slipped her fingers inside Emma and began to plunge them in and out. Emma purred with delight. Her fingers still working away, Lillian bent over and stuck her head between Emma's thighs. She snaked her tongue down to Emma's nub, licking, sucking, flicking.

"Oh god…" Emma writhed on the desk, her hands scrabbling at the wood desktop, the fire deep within her growing stronger.

"Lillian." Emma straightened up and lifted Lillian's face back up to kiss her. She wanted Lillian inside her, and against her, and all around her at once.

Lillian drew Emma close with her free hand. Emma wrapped her thighs around Lillian's hips, clinging onto Lillian's shoulders as she speared, harder, faster, deeper. They lost themselves in a haze of passion, their bodies becoming indistinguishable from each other.

"Lillian…" Emma's pleasure crested, then surged through her whole body. She bucked against Lillian, riding out the swift, relentless orgasm. Lillian smothered Emma's wild cry with her lips.

Emma's body stilled, and her grip on Lillian's blouse

loosened, but she didn't let go. Lillian didn't stop kissing her until both of them had to come up for air.

A contented murmur arose from Emma's chest. "I've changed my mind," Emma said. "I don't want to stop working for you anymore. Not if it means more of this."

Lillian smiled. "Don't say that, or I'll be tempted to keep you here, all to myself, forever."

"I wouldn't mind if you did," Emma said. "Keep me forever, I mean."

Lillian planted a light, lingering kiss on Emma's lips. "Emma," she said. "I'm never, ever going to let you go."

EPILOGUE

EMMA

*E*mma left the hospital after the first day of her new job. She'd spent the past two years cramming in all the required coursework so that she could get her degree, and as of this morning, she was officially employed as a social worker at one of the biggest hospitals in the city. Today had mostly been orientation and paperwork. She couldn't wait to start for real.

As Emma walked to her car, she took her phone out of her purse. She hadn't looked at it since lunchtime. Sure enough, there was a message from Lillian.

I hope your first day is going well. Let me know when you're on your way home, it read. The message had been sent an hour ago.

I'm leaving now, Emma wrote back. Surely Lillian would still be at work. *Why?*

Lillian's reply was instant. *I thought we could celebrate your first day. See you soon.*

Emma smiled. She rarely got to spend the whole evening with Lillian on a weeknight. Lillian's firm was booming, and she'd picked up some pro-bono work, so she had her hands full. Emma didn't mind. Seeing how happy Lillian's work made her was enough for Emma. And Lillian more than made up for it on weekends, which she reserved for the two of them.

She wondered what Lillian had planned. An evening out at a nice restaurant? A night at home, cuddling on the couch and watching movies? Either would have made her happy. She was a woman of simple pleasures. All that mattered was that Lillian was with her.

A half hour in traffic later, Emma reached their apartment. The two of them had moved in together soon after Lillian had opened her firm. Emma parked her car and rode the elevator up to their apartment.

She unlocked the door and opened it wide. "Lillian? I'm home."

She looked through the doorway and gasped. The lights were off, the hallway lit by what had to be a hundred candles. At her feet was a trail of pink, white, and red rose petals leading to their bedroom. Emma followed it, looking around in awe as she walked.

She crossed into their bedroom. At the end of the trail of petals was a ring of candles. And standing in the middle of it was Lillian. Emma's heart fluttered. She felt exactly like she had the moment Lillian had walked into her office on her first day at AG&W.

"Lillian? What's all this?" Emma asked.

"This is me showing you how much I love you," Lillian said. "This is me telling you that I want to be with you forever. This is me giving you that fairytale ending you deserve."

"Lillian…"

Lillian got down on one knee and took Emma's hand. With her other hand, she produced a small silver diamond ring.

"Will you marry me, Emma?"

Emma's heart stopped. "Is that…" She looked at the ring between Lillian's fingers. "Is that my mom's wedding ring?"

Lillian nodded.

"How?"

"She gave it to me months ago. She wanted you to have it."

"My dad gave that to her." All at once, Emma's emotions began to overflow. Tears ran down her cheeks.

"Emma?" Lillian stood up and took Emma's hands. "I'm sorry, I didn't mean to upset you."

Emma let out a sob. "I'm not upset. I'm happy. It's perfect."

"Is that a yes, then?"

Emma laughed. "Of course, Lillian. Yes."

With a smile, Lillian slipped the ring on Emma's finger.

Emma sniffed and wiped her eyes. "I must look like a mess right now."

"You look beautiful." Lillian reached out and wiped away a tear from Emma's cheek. "As always."

"You're my girlfriend. You have to say that."

"That's where you're wrong. I'm your fiancée. And I'm just being honest."

"I'm your fiancée…" Emma looked at the ring on her finger in disbelief. "We're getting married! And you did all of this?" She gestured at the candles and rose petals on the floor. "It's so perfect."

"I'm glad you think so," Lillian said. "I wondered if it was too cliché."

"It's very cliché. But that's why I love it." Emma kissed Lillian on the lips.

"Now we have another reason to celebrate tonight. I made a reservation for two at that Italian place you love. Unless you'd rather stay in?"

Emma shook her head. "Let's go out."

"I was hoping you'd say that," Lillian said. "Why hide you away when I can show you off to the whole world?"

ABOUT THE AUTHOR

Anna Stone is the bestselling author of Being Hers. Her
lesbian romance novels are sweet, passionate, and sizzle
with heat. When she isn't writing, Anna can usually be
found relaxing on the beach with a book.
Anna currently lives on the sunny east coast of Australia.

Visit www.annastoneauthor.com for information on her
books and to sign up for her newsletter.

 facebook.com/AnnaStoneRomance
twitter.com/AnnaStoneAuthor

Made in the USA
Monee, IL
12 February 2020

21671180R00143